WANTED: ONE WEDDING DRESS

**Three brides in search
of the perfect dress—
and the perfect husband!**

Welcome to this fabulous new trilogy by
talented Presents™ author Sharon Kendrick.
On a bride's special day, there's nothing
more important to her than a beautiful
wedding dress—apart from the perfect
bridegroom! Meet three women who are
about to find both....

This month in **One Wedding Required!**,
Amber wears the very same dress that
Holly Lovelace wore in
One Bridegroom Required!

And don't miss **One Husband Required!**
in April (Harlequin Presents® #2023),
when Amber's sister, Ursula, walks up
the aisle in it, too!

Read on and share the excitement as
Holly, Amber and Ursula meet and marry
their bridegrooms!

Dear Reader,

Planning a wedding is like writing your first book—you should stick with what you know! My husband and I were flat broke when we got married, and the only way to guarantee a show-stopping dress was to have it made for me (refusing to accept that my curvy shape looked nothing like the supermodel on the front of the pattern!). So I bought slippery satin and filmy organza and the dress was made and...

And I looked like a whale!

Two weeks before the ceremony, I had to rush out to buy a replacement dress. Luckily I found one—but I ended up with two wedding dresses and a lot of extra expense!

With weddings, it's best to play safe....

At least until after the service is over!

Sharon Kendrick

SHARON KENDRICK

One Wedding Required!

WANTED: ONE
WEDDING DRESS

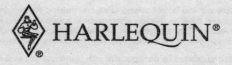

HARLEQUIN®

TORONTO • NEW YORK • LONDON
AMSTERDAM • PARIS • SYDNEY • HAMBURG
STOCKHOLM • ATHENS • TOKYO • MILAN • MADRID
PRAGUE • WARSAW • BUDAPEST • AUCKLAND

To legal-eagle Catrin, honey-voiced Hyim,
and their three gorgeous children,
Naomi, David and Daniella

ISBN 0-373-12017-6

ONE WEDDING REQUIRED!

First North American Publication 1999.

Copyright © 1999 by Sharon Kendrick.

PROLOGUE

THE wedding dress gleamed indistinctly through its heavy shrouding of plastic.

It was an exquisite gown—simple and striking and fashioned with care from ivory silk-satin. Organza whispered softly beneath the skirt and the matching veil was made of gossamer-fine tulle.

At a little over twenty years old, it was ageless and timeless, a future heirloom—to be passed down from bride to bride, each woman adapting it and making it uniquely hers.

The dress already had a history. It had been worn once, by Holly Lovelace, but it had originally been bought for the weddings of two other women: two sisters.

One of those sisters was Amber O'Neil, and it was her destiny to wear that dress.

But everyone knew the many twists and turns that destiny could take…

CHAPTER ONE

'SO, AMBER—' the journalist looked up from his notebook and smiled at her encouragingly '—can you tell us the story of how you and Finn Fitzgerald actually *met*?'

Amber hesitated, the question making her uncomfortably aware that she was breaking an unspoken rule. This wasn't the kind of thing she normally did. She never gave interviews. Neither did Finn. Never allowed cameras inside their home either, and yet she had done just that today. Then had spent the afternoon changing into a variety of outfits and striking a number of different poses all around their home.

There had been Amber in black satin, reclining against huge white cushions on their king-size bed. Amber in a pink cashmere dress, her hair tucked neatly behind her ear, while she pretended to talk into the telephone. Amber in jeans, drinking juice and swinging her legs from the kitchen counter. And, of course, Amber wrinkling her nose at the photographer as she stood in front of the scarlet-ribboned Christmas garlands the journalist had brought with him to decorate her mantelpiece. She was to be in the pre-Christmas edition of the magazine, which they were shooting several weeks before the festival itself—and therefore they had to manufacture an early Christmas.

Amber didn't mind a bit. Christmas was one of her favourite times of year—a time when she always went rather mad. She had needed very little persuasion to put the tree up a few weeks earlier than she would normally have done. After all, the shops had had them in their windows for weeks and weeks!

The photographer had got quite excited as he gazed into his viewfinder, telling her that the subtle gleam of her golden dress contrasted beautifully against the dark green of the pine needles.

They had wanted to shoot her standing in the garden, wearing a filmy dress, but, apart from the fact that the weather was too cold, Amber knew that trick of old. They would take the shot and carefully use the position of the sun to ensure that the dress ended up looking entirely see-through. Her body would be on show for all the world to see—as surely as if she were naked!

And while Amber still wasn't sure what Finn's reaction to this article would be, she knew damn well that he would draw the line at that! For a man who worked in an industry where nudity barely caused a flicker of consternation, Finn Fitzgerald was curiously old-fashioned when it came to his fiancée.

Fiancée!

Amber swallowed down her excitement, and allowed her gaze to drift to the whacking great stone which glittered so brilliantly on the third finger of her left hand. It was still hard to believe, but the engagement ring was solid and real, and confirmation enough. She was engaged to be married to Finn Fitzgerald—the man she loved with a passion which terrified her. The man of her dreams. The man...

'Amber?'

'Mmm?' Amber looked up and stared back at the journalist who had broken into her reverie, her dark blue eyes first blinking, then focussing as she forced her thoughts back to the present.

'You were saying?' he prompted, with all the smoothness of the professional interrogator.

Amber blinked. 'I was?'

'About Finn. And how you met.'

'Oh.' Amber smiled. *'That!'* Well, what the hell? Why *not* tell their story to the world? Finn had given her the biggest diamond ring she had ever seen—so he obviously didn't mind the whole world knowing that they were engaged. And in fact a big part of Amber *wanted* to tell the world. Wanted to cause something of a stir.

Because after Finn had slipped the ring on her finger, Amber had been aware of a curious feeling of deflation, of anticlimax. As though the engagement should have changed everything between them—and yet everything seemed exactly as it had been before. Was that usual for engaged couples? she found herself wondering worriedly. And was it right?

'How did I meet Finn?' Amber mused aloud, in answer to the journalist's searching stare. 'Well, it was nothing really *special*. No, let me put that another way— it *was* very special, of course it was, but...' Her voice tailed off and she bit her lip, wondering just how to put into words the physical and mental and psychological impact of falling in love at first sight with a man like Finn. A man who regularly bowled women over like ninepins.

The journalist held up his hand as he fiddled around with the tape recorder, then cleared his throat. 'Tell you what—' his smile was fulsome '—why don't we have a drink while we talk?'

'A drink? What—like tea?'

The man gave a cynical laugh. 'Ever met a journalist who drinks tea? I was thinking more on the lines of wine!'

'In the middle of the afternoon?'

The man shrugged, thinking that, for such a babe, she was pretty naive. 'We won't be breaking any laws.

That's why I brought the bubbly with me.' He pointed to the frosted and expensive bottle. 'To celebrate your engagement.'

Amber nodded, absurdly pleased—but then her new status as Finn's wife-to-be was still too novel for her to behave in a way which could be described as *normal*! Did newly engaged women drink champagne in the middle of the afternoon with men who were strangers? The journalist obviously thought so. 'Okay, Mr Millington,' she agreed with a smile. 'Why not?'

The journalist, 'call me Paul', took over the task of opening the champagne and pouring two glassfuls with the speed of a man who had performed this particular task many times before.

'To your future happiness,' he told her rather insincerely, as they touched glasses.

It sounded like a bell ringing as crystal chinked against crystal. Wedding bells, thought Amber suddenly. She *definitely* wanted wedding bells. A nice old-fashioned wedding. It didn't have to be big, but it had to be in a church—not a trendy rush to some upmarket London register office! But they hadn't even discussed the wedding properly. Not once. And she found herself wondering whether *that* was right, too.

'Cheers!' said Paul. He drank deeply and switched his tape recorder back on. 'Now, fire away. Tell me how it all started. You wanted to be a model, right?'

Amber shook her head. 'Not really, no. It certainly wasn't something I set out to do.'

'But all your life people had been telling you that you were beautiful, right?'

'Wrong.' Amber shook her head again ruefully. 'I didn't grow up in that sort of world. I lived in a rough part of London on a big, sprawling estate—'

The journalist expelled a long breath of surprise. He

would never have guessed it, not in a million years. With the Dresden delicacy of her looks, she looked like a woman who had been born and brought up in the lap of luxury—waited on and fêted all her life. 'Really?'

'Really.' Amber sipped her wine, almost amused by the shock which had registered on his face. 'My mother was a widow, and money was very tight. She'd worked her fingers to the bone to bring me and my sister up in a pretty hostile world. And in that world, good looks were dangerous.'

'Dangerous?' The journalist looked at her with interest, sniffing out a different angle on an old story.

Amber nodded, the memories crowding in fast now, demanding to be heard. Painful memories. Her mother's old-fashioned reluctance to talk to her daughters about growing up and sex. The shock of Amber's periods starting, and the unfamiliarity of her fast-burgeoning breasts. She had been too frightened to ask her mother to buy her a bra, and even more frightened by the raw gleam of desire she'd seen reflected in the eyes of the men who had lived in the council flats around her.

'It was the kind of world where girls of sixteen got pregnant, then deserted. Jobs were scarce and men were fickle. Easy come. Easy go. A pretty face meant that you had to fight them off.' Particularly if that pretty face was outstanding in its prettiness.

Amber had quickly learnt to minimise her assets. Hair scraped back. No make-up. Clothes worn to disguise a body rather than to draw attention to it. While Amber's contemporaries had been squeezing themselves into tight, tight jeans and clinging tops, Amber had been dressing in the kind of clothes which would have looked good in a maternity department. Her sister Ursula had used a different method of concealment—she had just got fat.

'Did you ever get fed up with fighting them off?' asked Paul slyly.

Amber laughed. 'Never. And I never let them get close enough to *have* to fight them off. I just knew that there was something better out there. A different kind of life. The flat we lived in was poky—far too small for my mother and sister and me. So I left there just as soon as I could—at sixteen.'

Paul nodded. 'With qualifications?'

Amber shook her head. 'You're joking! The school I went to wasn't famous for getting its pupils through exams.' Her voice was wry. 'If it kept them out of the remand centres and off the streets, it considered that it had done a good job!'

Paul scanned the sheet of paper in front of him. 'But you didn't join the Allure agency until you were almost twenty, right?'

'Right.'

'So what does a girl of sixteen with no qualifications do?'

'She gets a job living in. Hotels, usually. You can always find a job in a hotel. I've been a chambermaid and a receptionist. I've worked behind bars and I've waited tables. The money is lousy, but at least you can get yourself a room in central London.'

'Smart girl.' The journalist refilled his glass. 'And you made the most of the city, did you?'

I tried. I did everything that was free—so I knew all the art galleries and museums like the back of my hand.'

'Exciting times,' murmured the journalist sarcastically.

'Those bits I loved,' Amber defended staunchly. 'And I started reading, too. Devouring books which filled in the education I'd missed.'

'Then what?'

Amber shrugged. 'Too many people kept telling me that I had a beautiful face—'

'And that was a problem?'

She shook her head. 'No, of course it wasn't a problem—I'd grown up seeing *real* problems, and having a sympathetically proportioned face certainly didn't qualify! But after a while it becomes a little difficult to ignore, especially when the novelty of having your own place wears off. The hours at the hotel were long and tedious, and the money was lousy, and all of a sudden my poky little room began to look less like a palace and more of a prison.' And there had been more men to fight off. Rich, slick businessmen whose rooms she'd cleaned, who'd thought that their fat wallets and fat stomachs would make them appealing to a young girl with only her looks and her natural intelligence as assets.

The whirr of the tape recorder was the only sound in the room. It was a hypnotic sound. 'Go on,' said Paul smoothly.

It was strangely cathartic to be able to talk so honestly about her past. Amber narrowed her navy eyes and let the words come spilling out, shuddering as she remembered the corpulent company director who had asked her to become his mistress!

'I found myself looking into the future,' she said slowly. 'And I realised that, if I wasn't careful, then I was consigning myself to a life of drudgery just like my mother's had been. Only things were different for me. I wasn't a widow with two children—I didn't *have* to live like that. I was limiting my horizons for no other reason than that I feared my attraction to the opposite sex.'

The journalist gave a cynical laugh. 'So you really threw yourself in at the deep end by getting hooked up to a man like Finn Fitzgerald?'

Amber shook her head. 'I didn't get "hooked up"

tos, then I would probably make a reasonable amount of money—'

The journalist frowned. 'I don't understand.'

'Neither did I, at first. It was his idea of a joke, you see. Implying that I looked like…like…'

'Like?'

'A streetwalker,' she admitted reluctantly.

'He said *that*?'

'Implied that.'

'So what did *you* say?'

'I told him that his eyes looked like traffic lights—'

'*Traffic* lights?'

Amber giggled. 'Well, yes. His eyes are green, you see—very, very green—only this time they were red as well. He'd had a terrible bout of flu, apparently—first time he'd ever been sick in his adult life. Everyone there said what a terrible patient he had made.'

'I can't imagine anyone saying something negative about Finn Fitzgerald's looks. That must have been a first. Did he mind?'

'No. He laughed. Just threw back his head and laughed, and said, *"Touché,"* and everyone stopped what they were doing and just stared at me. At first I thought they were staring because I must have looked such a state. It wasn't until much later that they told me they had been amazed to see Finn laughing so uninhibitedly. They nicknamed him "Grin" Fitzgerald for a while after that, until he put a stop to it.'

'You mean he's a sourpuss usually?'

'I don't know if I'd put it *quite* that way. I mean that not many people can make him laugh.'

'But you can?'

Amber let her gaze fall demurely to her lap. 'I hope so.'

'So he signed you up and asked you out?'

Amber shook her head. 'No. He told me that I wasn't tall enough to be a model.'

The journalist let his eyes roam over her. She looked pretty damn good from where he was sitting. 'Aren't you?'

'Not really. I'm just over five seven, and most models top six foot these days.'

'What did you say?'

'I told him he wasn't polite enough to be my boss, anyway. And that made him laugh. Again.'

'So you left?'

Amber shook her head. 'I was about to. Then a phone rang and he started speaking into it, and another one rang and he started gesturing impatiently with his hand, so I picked it up and answered it. I took a message and wrote it down and then started walking out.'

'So then what happened?'

'He called me back and asked if I could type and I told him that I could, after a fashion. Then he asked if I could make coffee and I said yes, could he?'

'And he laughed again, right?'

Amber smiled. 'That's right.'

'Then what?'

'Then he offered me a job.'

'As?'

'A general dogsbody, really—only he gave it a fancy name.'

'And you told him what he could do with his job?'

'I was very tempted,' admitted Amber. And not just by the job, either. 'But intrigued, at the same time. The atmosphere in this place was wild. And buzzy. I told him that I'd think about it and he said that he didn't have time to discuss it then, but would I meet him later that evening?'

'And he took you out for dinner, right?'

'That's right,' smiled Amber. 'But he brought two models along with him.'

'So it wasn't the romantic evening of a lifetime?'

'Not at all. These two women spent their time being bitchy to one another and trying to compete for his attention.'

'And what did you do?'

'I let them get on with it. Just sat there enjoying my supper.'

'And he was surprised?'

'Amazed. First of all he sent the two models home, then he looked at my empty plate and said he'd never seen a woman put away that much food before. And I told him that was because I didn't get to eat in restaurants like that every day, and if he didn't appreciate the yummy things on the menu then maybe his palate was jaded and perhaps he should try a diet of simple food for a while.'

'And he laughed again, right?'

'Yes, he did. And he asked me whether I could cook and I told him that, yes, of course I could cook—but was he looking for an assistant or a wife?'

'Let me guess—he stared into your big blue eyes and said it was the latter and he'd been waiting all his life for a girl like you?'

'He did not. He frowned at me and told me that if I went to work for him I'd have to do something about my image, and I said, "Like *what*?" So he told me to report to him first thing the following morning and all would be revealed.' Amber took another mouthful of wine, really enjoying herself now. Thinking what uncomplicated fun it had been back then. 'So I turned to him and asked, "Does this mean you're offering me the job?" and he glared at me and said of course it did.'

'So you jumped for joy?'

'I did not. I told him that I couldn't accept a job unless there was accommodation involved, because my job at the hotel was a living-in job. And he said that shouldn't be a problem—that he could find me accommodation.'

'Meaning you could move in with him, I suppose, which was where love first blossomed?'

Amber shook her head. 'Oh, no. He was offering me the grotty old flat above the agency—well, I say grotty. It wasn't *that* bad, and Finn had it decorated for me.' She remembered how he had insisted on choosing the colours and how it had rankled. Colours which would not have been *her* choice at all. But in the end it seemed that Finn had known best, because Amber had grown to love the decor he had picked out. As in so many other areas of her life, he had been her guide and her mentor. 'So I moved in.'

The journalist licked his lips. 'And he joined you?'

Amber shook her head and laughed. 'Oh, no! I couldn't have imagined Finn living there! *He* had a much grander apartment overlooking Hyde Park.'

The journalist looked around him. 'That's *this* apartment?'

Amber nodded. 'Uh-huh—and eventually I moved in *here*. With him. But that's how it all started.'

The journalist swallowed down another mouthful of wine. 'So it was like—a red-hot romance straight away?'

'Certainly not!' Amber's mouth pursed into a prim little line. 'I worked for Finn for two years before he even laid a finger on me.' Until she had grown to want him so much that she'd thought she would die with the wanting. And had convinced herself that a man like that wouldn't look twice at a working-class girl from the council estate. But in that she had been completely wrong. A smile played around the lush curves of her mouth. 'He played *Pygmalion* instead.'

'And how did he do that?' asked the journalist casually.

'Oh, he sent me to a make-up artist and a hairdresser. Then I had my colours done by a colour therapist, and after that I saw a stylist and she advised me about what kind of clothes to wear.'

'She advised you pretty well,' murmured the journalist, running his eyes over the gold silk-knitted tunic dress she wore, which showed off the best pair of legs he had ever seen.

'Well, Finn certainly thinks so,' said Amber, an unmistakable note of reproof in her voice which told the journalist in no uncertain terms to back off.

'Er, yes. Finn.' Averting his eyes from the milky-white stockings which made her legs sheen so provocatively, the journalist took another sip of his champagne instead. 'He's doing pretty well for himself.'

Amber nodded. Sometimes she thought he was doing a little *too* well. The business was booming—and so successful that Finn rarely seemed to have time to draw breath just lately. Even acquiring a partner hadn't helped, not really—even though Jackson Geering was a faultless choice. In fact, maybe Jackson was just *too* good.

He had been taken on by Finn to ease some of the workload at Allure—but such was Jackson's talent for the business that he had succeeded in drumming up a whole load of new openings! He was currently in New York, looking into the possibility of opening a branch of Allure over there. Amber knew that Finn was excited by the prospect and she was worried. How far did a man have to drive himself before he could accept his own success?

But, while she might suggest that he was in danger of

overdosing on stress, she couldn't tell a man of nearly thirty-four how to live his life...

She sneaked a quick glance at her watch. It was getting on for five o'clock. And once Paul Millington had left she would be free to start cooking, which she loved so much that Finn often teased her about it. She liked to prepare robust food—full of vegetables and pulses. Hearty, healthy, economical meals, and, even though Finn told her time and time again that they were rich enough to eat caviare non-stop if they wanted to, some part of her loved concocting the simple meals which had been a part of both their childhoods.

The journalist saw her looking at her watch, recognising that she wanted to end the interview. Good. When the subject was impatient for him to leave, that was when they were often at their most indiscreet. And indiscretions made the best stories, no doubt about it...

'So how did Finn propose?'

Amber laughed and shook her head, the thick hair swaying as fluidly as golden syrup. 'Oh, no—I'm not falling for *that* one! He'd kill me if I told you!'

'In bed, then?' he quizzed mischievously.

Amber blushed like a thousand sunrises, and then could have kicked herself. 'I'm not saying!'

Actually, they *hadn't* been in bed at the time. They had been closeted in a sumptuous downstairs bathroom at a weekend house party which neither of them had really wanted to attend, hosted by the owner of one of the country's best-selling glossy magazines.

Finn rarely did anything he didn't want to do, and he didn't like socialising much. For a start, he didn't get the time. And when he did he liked to live a simple life, far away from the glamour of the industry in which he worked. But even Finn had been able to see the sense of attending such a party.

'Shall we go?' he had queried casually one morning as they had been driving in to work together.

'Do we *have* to go?' Amber had asked.

She still felt shy in the company of huge gatherings of strangers—probably because most people were captivated by Finn. *He* was the one they wanted to talk to, not her. For all her blue-eyed, golden-haired beauty, people still gravitated to the dark man with the streetwise eyes by her side. Sometimes, Amber felt like a dim satellite next to Finn's bright, blazing planet.

Finn shook his head. 'We don't *have* to do anything, sweetheart—but it might be fun.'

'*Fun?*'

'Mmm. Show you the sort of life we *could* be living.'

As an exercise in comparison, it proved invaluable, showing Amber—if she had needed showing—that the glossy high life was not for her.

She was forced to put up with beautiful women flirting outrageously with Finn all evening, acting for all the world as though he had not brought a woman with him.

He saw her resigned expression across the table as she picked at her smoked salmon, and attracted her attention without too much trouble, leaning across the table to talk to her.

'What's up?' he quizzed softly.

Amber shrugged. 'Nothing.'

'Something,' he contradicted. 'Is it the other women?'

She gave him a rueful smile. 'It goes with the territory, Finn—you're an extremely attractive man, and they just can't seem to stop themselves!'

'No,' he agreed thoughtfully, his dark lashes framing the emerald brightness of his eyes. 'But maybe you think I encourage them?'

'No.'

'Even subconsciously?'

She shook her head. 'You don't need to have legions of women fawning over you in order to boost your self-esteem—your ego is healthy enough without that!' But maybe she ought to make more of an effort to enjoy herself in a similar way. 'Go back to your fan club, Finn Fitzgerald,' she told him softly. 'I'm fine.'

She forced herself to chat to the man on her right—a wunderkind film director who, she soon discovered, had an irreverent sense of humour. Even though she was aware of the beauty busy pouting beside Finn, the wunderkind managed to keep her halfway entertained all the way through the impressive array of different courses. She was just unwrapping another chocolate mint when she glanced up to find Finn looking at her very intently.

She put the mint down, untasted, and leaned across the table towards him. 'Is something wrong, Finn?'

'Meet me downstairs,' he urged her suddenly.

Amber blinked. 'Why?'

He shook his head and his green eyes glittered. 'No questions.'

'Not even to ask where?'

He laughed. 'Why don't you hide in one of the shadowed recesses in the hallway,' he suggested in a sexy murmur, 'and let me come and find you?'

Her heart was beating very strongly with excitement as she rose to her feet, convinced that people must have guessed at their elaborate charade, but the wunderkind was now chatting to the woman on the other side of him, and no one else looked in her direction as she slipped away.

She went into one of the downstairs bathrooms, where she brushed her hair and washed her hands, and applied a faint lick of lipstick. She was just about to leave when Finn appeared in the doorway, a look of anticipation and excitement on his face as he came inside and silently closed and locked the door behind him.

'Finn?' Amber said breathlessly.

'Shh!' He took her into his arms and began to kiss her with a sweet determination which Amber knew could only mean one thing...

'Finn!' she protested breathily as he began to stroke her nipple absently with his thumb.

He eased her against the wall. 'What?' came the smoky reply.

'You mustn't.'

'Why mustn't I?'

'Because...' Amber's head tipped back helplessly as he began to anoint her neck with kisses. 'Because...'

'Lost for words?' he tormented sweetly, as his hand snaked possessively between her thighs, the silky fabric of her dress parting like magic for his fingers.

Lost, yes. Definitely. Lost in an inimitable sensual world of his making. She moulded her hands helplessly around his buttocks, feeling the hard ridge of his desire as he pressed willingly against her pelvis. 'We... we...shouldn't be doing this,' she gulped, as she felt him ruck the silky fabric up her legs.

'Why not?'

'Because people are upstairs—'

'So what?'

'W-what...?' Her voice trailed away with excitement as she heard the rasping of his zip. 'What if they guess?'

'Guess what?'

'That you're...you're...'

'I'm what?' He stared straight into her face, seeing her eyes dilate with shock and excitement as he pushed the lace panel of her panties aside and slowly eased himself into her molten tightness.

'Unscrupulous!' she gasped, as he began to move against her.

'And?'

'Gorgeous,' came her breathy admission, just as pleasure and excitement and guilt all combined to give her the most heart-stopping orgasm she could remember, and she knew from the sudden tension in his body that his was not far behind. She felt him shudder helplessly within the circle of her arms and she held him very tightly until the storm had subsided.

Afterwards they stood wrapped around each other, Amber's skin all pink and glowing as she yawned lazily against his neck, and he tilted her head to face him.

'I've been thinking—' he began.

'Oh, is *that* what you call it?' she teased him, her voice all slurred and satiated.

'About those women.'

'It doesn't matter.'

'Oh, but it does, sweetheart. It does. And it bothers you, doesn't it, Amber?'

She thought about it. 'Of course it bothers me,' she admitted carefully. 'I think it would bother most women—but I *hope* that I manage to conceal it well—'

'Not from me, you don't.'

'Well, from everyone else, then. I mean—it isn't as though I threw a tantrum at dinner and marched off to bed. I thought I hid my impatience fairly well.'

'You did,' he agreed softly, and kissed her tenderly on the tip of her nose. 'I only picked it up because I know you so well and I can recognise all the tell-tale signs.'

'And what are they?'

'It was when you ate that *fourth* after-dinner mint that I knew you were feeling tense!'

Amber giggled.

He pushed a wayward strand of golden hair off her flushed cheek. 'Although I noticed that you soon found yourself an interesting diversion,' he told her carefully.

Amber's heart hammered. 'I take it you're referring to the film director?'

'You know I am.'

Surely that wasn't *jealousy* colouring his voice? *Finn?* Jealous of *her*? It thrilled her almost as much as it shocked her. 'And did you mind?' Amber's voice was equally careful.

'I guess I did. Stupid, isn't it?'

'Not stupid.' She rested her head on his shoulder. 'It's natural to feel jealous—even when you know that your fears are groundless.'

'I guess so.' He planted a kiss on the silky curtain of her hair and Amber raised her head reluctantly.

'Do we *have* to go back up there, Finn? From the predatory gleam in the eyes of some of those women, they'll probably suggest throwing car keys into the middle of the room! Quite apart from the fact that I feel a little...' she met his eyes, and blushed '...*sticky*.'

'Me, too.' He smiled back at her.

'So do you suppose we could get away with sneaking off to our room and hope that no one will notice?'

He shook his head and Amber noticed that he looked oddly keyed up. 'Not yet. I've got something I want to say to you first.'

She looked around the gleaming bathroom and wondered if a queue might be gathering outside, until she remembered that there were probably more bathrooms than guests in a house this size! Still, as an environment for talking, it *did* leave a little to be desired! 'Can't it wait?'

'No, sweetheart. I'm afraid it can't.'

Amber raised her eyebrows quizzically, as some gritty

quality in his voice alerted her to the fact that this was not your average run-of-the-mill post-coital chat. 'Sounds ominous.'

'Does it? I hope not.' He lifted a shiny strand of amber hair and twisted it around his finger. 'These women that come on to me—they don't exactly show you any respect, do they, sweetheart?'

She gave a hollow laugh. 'Not exactly, no!'

'And maybe that's because they think that you're just a girlfriend—'

'*Just?*' she interrupted indignantly. 'What's that supposed to mean?'

'Kind of impermanent, I suppose,' he observed slowly.

'But we've been living together for almost two years!'

'But *they're* not to know that, are they?' he questioned patiently. 'They probably don't think we've made any kind of commitment to each other.'

'Well, that's true. We haven't,' she pointed out truthfully. 'But lots of people don't—not these days. And it's not as though I *mind*,' she added hastily.

'I know you don't—but suddenly I *do* mind. I mind very much. And I want to do something about it.'

'You're talking in riddles, Finn Fitzgerald,' she chided gently. 'And it isn't at all like you.'

'Well, I'm a bit of a novice at this kind of thing.' He grinned.

Amber blinked. 'And what kind of thing is that?'

His eyes darkened and, when he spoke, his voice sounded so husky that he didn't sound like Finn at all. 'Proposals of marriage—that kind of thing.'

'Pro-proposals of *marriage*?' she echoed incredulously.

'Do you want to?'

'What?' She needed to hear him say it out loud, because half of her wondered whether she wasn't just dreaming the whole thing up.

'Marry me?'

Her heart stilled with disbelieving joy and she didn't stop to question his intent for a second, because there was one thing she knew about Finn—and that was that he *never* said things he didn't mean.

'Oh, Finn,' she whispered ecstatically. 'My gorgeous, gorgeous Finn! How can you ask me a question like that? Of *course* I want to marry you!'

And it wasn't until they had stopped kissing that he withdrew a small leather box from his pocket, and Amber's eyes widened with amazement to see that it contained a diamond ring which fitted her finger perfectly when he slid it on.

'Good heavens!' she squealed, as it sparkled like a starburst. 'It's the biggest diamond I've ever seen!'

'That should keep predatory women away in future,' he growled. 'Do you like it?'

'Don't ask such idiotic questions! Of course I like it— I love it! But it *fits*! And fits so well!'

'So?'

'So you mean you had this whole proposal thing planned?'

He gave her a slow smile. 'Now who's asking the idiotic questions? Of course I did! Or do you imagine I'd leave something as important as marriage just to whim?'

'So you went out—and *bought* the ring?'

'Well, I sure as hell didn't steal it,' he teased.

'You guessed my size?'

He shook his head. 'I borrowed that tiny moonstone thing you wear. I took it from the dressing table weeks ago.'

'And I thought I'd lost it!'

And their eyes met in a long moment.

'I love you,' he said simply.

'Snap,' she told him shakily.

'Amber? *Amber?*'

Lost in her reverie, Amber looked up to find the journalist staring at her.

His eyes were hard, but his words were casual—casual enough to lull her into a false sense of security. 'So where *exactly* did he propose?'

His question seeped insidiously into the mists of her consciousness, and Amber heard herself saying automatically, 'In the bathroom—of all places!'

'The *bathroom*?'

'Yes, but I don't really want to answer any more questions, certainly not on *that*—would you mind?'

The journalist gave a contented smirk as he shook his head. He had a pretty good idea of what must have happened in the bathroom—she had one of those beautifully transparent faces that were a huge boon to his job! 'Of course I don't mind.' He twirled his pencil in between his thumb and forefinger and drew in a deep breath as he psyched himself up to ask what he always termed his face-slapping question. Though, come to think of it, Amber O'Neil—despite her fiery golden hair—looked far too much of a lady ever to slap him round the face— no matter *what* the provocation!

'You're a good-looking woman, Amber—'

'Why, thank you,' she put in drily. 'Very nice of you to say so!'

'But you work in an industry peopled with beautiful women, some who—dare I say it?—are far more beautiful than you.'

Amber's voice was wry. 'Oh, you can say it, Mr Millington—'

'Paul.'

'Paul,' Amber echoed obediently, and smiled. 'Other people have said it before, time and again.'

'So will you share with our readers the secret of your mystery *weapon*?'

'The weapon with which I entrapped Finn, you mean?'

'Exactly!'

His eyes glinted rather insultingly and Amber knew exactly what he was not-so-subtly implying. What did the man expect, for heaven's sake? That she was going to suddenly announce that she was pure dynamite in bed? *That*, surely, was a testimony which only Finn could give...

'I have no secret weapon,' she told him quietly. 'The very word suggests conflict, and—so far—there has been remarkably little of that in our relationship. Touch wood,' she added superstitiously. 'Whatever works between us I think is down to one thing, pure and simple. Love,' she explained, in answer to his puzzled expression.

'Oh.' He looked positively crestfallen, and Amber almost felt sorry for him until she caught a glimpse of the time.

'I really ought to wind this up now,' she told him apologetically. 'If there are no more questions...?'

He smiled. 'Just one.'

Amber blinked at him, the curving sweep of her dark lashes beautifully framing the deep blue of her eyes. 'Oh?'

'It's the obvious one, really—when's the wedding going to be?'

If only she knew! 'Well, Finn mentioned Valentine's Day in passing, but I'm not sure whether we'll get it organised for then. It's only a couple of months away.'

The journalist's eyes gleamed like twin beacons. 'A

Valentine's Day wedding!' he breathed. 'It would make a wonderful piece. Front-page spread,' he added, a sly light gleaming in his eyes. 'I can promise you that!'

Amber rose to her feet. Not with Finn co-operating, she would wager!

She felt vaguely uneasy as she showed Paul Millington out, but reasoned that he couldn't write anything *too* racy. Apart from those last few comments, she hadn't said anything that people didn't already know. And there wasn't much of a story about someone having been proposed to in a bathroom, was there? Not much of a scoop *there*!

She was humming gently to herself as she began to chop onions in preparation for making Finn's dinner.

CHAPTER TWO

FINN was delayed.

After the journalist had left, Amber kept glancing up at the clock as she chopped garlic and fresh coriander, wondering where her busy man had got to. He was often held up, but he usually let her know when he was going to be late.

Eventually he rang her on his mobile phone from the car, his voice faint and indistinct.

'Amber?'

'Where are you?'

'I've been tied up with New York,' he told her tiredly. 'Karolina Lindberg has been throwing tantrums and they've—' There was a loud crackling on the line and then a long squeak. Amber could hear the impatience in Finn's voice as he said, 'Listen, I'll tell you all about it when I get home, sweetheart, but I'm snarled up in traffic right now—'

'Okay,' murmured Amber, holding her hand up in the air, and watching while the hall light glittered and sparkled on the facets of her diamond ring. 'Drive carefully.'

'Don't I always?'

'No, you drive too fast!'

'Nag, nag, nag!' he laughed, and cut the connection.

She put the phone down, turned the chicken off and made herself a cup of tea, then settled down to read a magazine whilst trying not to look as though she was waiting—though of course she *was* waiting. Waiting for Finn, just as she always waited for Finn. But what choice did she have? He was a busy man, his business interests

31

were diverse, and, although she worked for Allure as well, she couldn't stay beside him *all* the time.

It was a side of herself that she had grown to dislike and fear—the side that didn't feel complete unless Finn was somewhere around, as though a major part of her was missing. Though that much, she supposed, was true. Finn *was* a major part of her life.

It just went against everything she believed in—that a woman simply couldn't function properly when she was on her own. That, although she was living, she simply didn't feel *alive* unless the tall, ruffle-haired man with the hard, lean body and the bright green eyes was somewhere in the vicinity.

She must have dozed off, something she never normally did, and awoke with a muzzy head to find Finn standing over her, his face pale and unsmiling.

She sat up immediately. 'Hello, darling,' she mumbled, and blinked at him rapidly while her eyes tried to accustom themselves to the overhead light he must have snapped on.

'Hard day?' he murmured sardonically.

'No.' Amber found herself frowning defensively. 'You knew I was taking the afternoon off—'

'I wasn't criticising you,' he said tetchily. 'Just that you couldn't have picked a worse day for it if you'd tried. The office has been going crazy—and it's never easy when Jackson is away.'

It wasn't like Finn to be this grouchy, and it contrasted so markedly with the cute version of their romance which she had given to the journalist that Amber felt a bit of a fool. 'Well, I wasn't to know that, was I?' she questioned sweetly. 'Not when I booked it last month, after your accountant specifically told me to take some of the holiday which was owing to me.'

'No, I guess not.' He tipped his head back and wearily rubbed the back of his neck.

'Hard day?' she asked him sympathetically.

'Tiring.' He pulled a face. 'I've had Birgitta on the phone from New York for most of the afternoon.'

'And just who is Birgitta?'

'She's Karolina Lindberg's mother. You met her— don't you remember? She's rather beautiful.'

Amber frowned. She met so many beautiful women every day of her life that she had sort of grown immune to them. But Finn, it would seem, had not. Not judging by the remark he had just made. It was his job to assess women on how they looked, but Amber found it oddly hurtful to hear the mother of one of his models described as 'rather beautiful'. She forced herself to put on an expression of interest. 'Tall? White-blonde hair? Used to be a model herself before she had Karolina?'

'That's the one!'

Amber forced herself to be generous. 'It's easy to see where Karolina got her beauty from.'

'She's a good-looking woman,' conceded Finn. 'They both are.'

Karolina was Finn's latest signing and one of Allure's biggest potential earners, a star in the making—the kind of woman who came around once every couple of years. If you were lucky.

It was difficult to pinpoint exactly what star quality was, but whatever it was Karolina had more than enough to go round. Six feet of exquisite white-blonde beauty, at sweet sixteen, she was a male fantasy come to life. Like her mother...

Amber narrowed her navy eyes, unaccustomed antennae alerted. 'And isn't there a *Mr* Lindberg on the scene?' she enquired casually.

Finn shook his head. 'Unfortunately, she's just separated from Karolina's father, and things are a little strained in the Lindberg family just now. Birgitta and Karolina are showing a distinct aversion to going back to Sweden. They've decided they want to be based in London.'

Amber felt unfamiliar fingers of fear whisper over her skin. 'And what's that got to do with you?'

'Well, they want to use the company flat, for starters.'

'Oh. I see.'

Like other leading model agencies, Allure owned a property solely for the use of its models—especially young and up-and-coming models, who needed a safe and cheap place to stay in the big city. For a nominal rent, the company flat could provide them with the security they needed. 'Karolina *and* her mother want to live there?' queried Amber. 'Isn't Birgitta a little old to be staying somewhere as basic as that?'

Finn shot her a narrow-eyed look and Amber thought how pale his face looked when contrasted against the dark hair. 'She's Karolina's chaperon.' He frowned. 'Where else are they going to stay? It's only Karolina's second job—she hasn't earned enough yet to put herself up in any of the London hotels. Not long-term. And you know how much they need reassurance and guidance at this stage, sweetheart.'

'And you give it them,' she observed.

'Well, that's all part of my job.'

'Sure.' Amber gave an automatic smile, but her heart felt unaccustomedly heavy. 'Just that sometimes I wish that *we* could have a little more time together, that's all.'

'You're wishing away our success?' he queried, a half-smile hovering around his lips. But it was a rueful smile.

Amber played with her engagement ring. 'I just wish

there was something in between having no work and having so much work you can't think straight.'

'But that's life, business.' He shrugged. 'It's all or nothing.'

He had struggled so hard to get to where he was today that Amber sometimes wondered whether he would be able to function normally *without* that struggle. Because Finn had had to fight every inch of the way to become the man he was today.

The youngest of seven children, Finn had come as a complete surprise to his brothers and sisters. And as a total shock to his mother—who had been in her late forties at the time of his birth and had thought her child-rearing days were over. She'd been too tired to cope with the dark-haired infant's vitality, so the afterthought had been brought up mainly by his eldest sister, Philomena—who had allowed him a lot more freedom than a strict mother might have done. As a consequence, Finn had grown used to quietly going about and getting what he wanted.

And what he'd wanted was success.

His good looks and natural grace had taken him out of the small Irish village of his birth and propelled him onto the international modelling scene like a rocket, at the age of eighteen—but he had soon tired of earning a living from his good looks. With a determination which was characteristic of the man, he had modelled when he could and laboured on the roads when he couldn't, and by the time he was twenty-five had saved enough money to start his own model agency.

He stifled a yawn. 'God, I need a drink.'

Normally Amber would have taken herself off and poured him one, but then normally he would have already taken her into his arms and kissed her very thoroughly indeed.

Which, so far, he hadn't. So far all he had talked about was Birgitta and Karolina.

'I wouldn't mind a drink myself,' she told him.

He blinked in surprise. 'Okay. Wine do you?'

The champagne had made her thirsty for a soft drink, but she wanted to go through the whole togetherness thing of sharing a bottle with Finn. Tonight she needed some reassurance of their closeness. 'Why not?' She smiled.

She followed him out into the kitchen and put some heat beneath the chicken and rice while Finn opened a bottle. He was just about to throw the cork away when he noticed the empty golden-foiled bottle of very expensive champagne which was lying in the bin.

He raised his eyebrows. 'Been celebrating?'

For some extraordinary reason Amber felt both defensive and indignant, though when she thought about it afterwards it was a question she might have asked herself, had the situation been reversed.

Though perhaps not with as much accusation in her voice.

'Not really,' she hedged, knowing his dislike of journalists and wondering what mad blip had possessed her to give an interview.

The dark eyebrows rose even higher. 'Just consuming costly bottles of champagne on your own?' he queried mildly.

'Well, of course I wasn't alone!' she retorted, guilt making her sound much snappier than usual. 'You must know by now that I'd never be able to drink that much on my own! Especially in the middle of the *day*!'

'I don't know anything, Amber,' he contradicted stubbornly. 'Since you seem determined to clothe your actions in secrecy.'

Amber's blue eyes widened into sapphire circles. If it

hadn't been so preposterous, it might almost have been funny, but she had never felt less like laughing. 'Clothe my actions in secrecy?' she repeated incredulously. 'Did you mean to sound like the lead role in a poor spy movie, Finn, or was it unintentional?'

'Damn you, Amber O'Neil!' he said softly. 'What the hell has been going on here today?'

This time she stared at him in utter confusion. What was happening? Why were they arguing? Why on earth was he *talking* to her like this? Suddenly Amber felt the shiver of misgivings as they trickled their way down her spine.

She had never known Finn be so prickly and confrontational. Oh, they had sparred often enough in the time they had been living together—and before that. Plenty of times. But humour and affection had lain behind *those* exchanges, while there was certainly no humour or affection lurking in the depths of Finn's emerald gaze right now.

She bit her lip and wondered how to answer him, because now did not seem the right time to tell him that she had sold the story of their meeting to *Wow!* magazine.

And he looked tired, too. Dog-tired. For the first time since he had arrived home Amber took a really close look at him—noting the blue-black shadows beneath his eyes and the tension around his jaw. His nerves were clearly jangled and stretched, and she frowned. He had been working too hard; that much was apparent. For where was the cool, calm Finn who coped equably with most things which were thrown at him?

'Ursula came round for a drink,' she told him, and offered a silent prayer of contrition for the lie. It was necessary, she told herself firmly. She would pick a better moment than this one to tell him the truth. A time when she was sure he would give her that easy, familiar laugh of his and tell her that, no, she shouldn't have done it—but that no real harm had been done.

'Ursula?' He frowned. 'Your *sister*?'

'I know only one Ursula.'

'What was Ursula doing round here in the middle of the day? Drinking champagne?'

Amber rounded on him. Enough was enough. 'There's no need to make it sound as though we were up to no good!' she told him furiously. 'Some of the women that work in Ursula's company go out to wine bars every single lunchtime!'

'And do absolutely zilch in the way of work afterwards, I'll bet!'

'But it was my afternoon off!' Amber pointed out, and to her horror she burst into tears.

Finn stared at her in amazement. 'Amber—'

'Shut up! Just shut up!' she sobbed, and ran from the kitchen towards the bedroom.

She flung herself down on the bed, her shoulders shaking with the effort of trying to keep the tears back, but it was no good. Great rivulets came streaking their way in a salty path down her nose and into her mouth and she swallowed them down like medicine. She was just scrubbing at her eyes and sniffing back the last of her tears when she heard the door open quietly, and Finn began to walk towards the bed.

She held her breath, froze into total stillness, her body language screaming out a wordless message of rejection. But it was a message which he was clearly choosing to ignore, for he put his hand on her shoulder.

She tried to shake it off. 'G-go away!'

'You know you don't want me to.'

'How do you know *what* I want?' she demanded.

'Why don't you tell me?' he suggested tenderly.

'Okay, I'll tell you!' She sat up on the bed, aware that she must look an absolute fright. Strands of golden hair were sticking to her cheeks like glue. 'I want a little respect, Finn Fitzgerald—that's what I want!' Then tell him the truth about this afternoon, a little voice inside her head urged her. She ignored it.

He sighed. 'Shall we start this evening all over again?'

'And how do you propose we do that?' she asked him quietly, but the instant the words were out of her mouth she realised that they could be interpreted as provocation.

His eyes briefly flickered, and Amber immediately recognised the dark, gleaming shutters of desire.

He smiled as he gave a shrug of his broad shoulders, clad in their habitual black. 'I don't know, Amber,' he murmured. 'Any ideas?'

She knew what he wanted. What *she* wanted, too, if she was being honest with herself. A sizzling session of making up, which would banish the memory of their angry words and make everything seem all right again. But she was damned if she was going to lie back on the bed and start giving him the come-on, pouting and desperate, with no pride.

She quickly got up off the bed, and Finn frowned.

'Where are you going?'

'To the kitchen. I've left the rice and chicken cooking. Remember?'

'So this is what an engagement means, is it?' he taunted softly. 'That you put supper before making love?'

Amber paused by the door, his words unsettling her. She found herself wanting to placate him, to run back over to the bed and start to massage the knotted tension from his shoulders in the way he so liked. And that would inevitably lead on to something else, in the way that massage always did. But that type of behaviour would consign her to a lifetime of being considered a doormat. She already had his supper ready and waiting for him every night—she sure as hell wasn't going to start agreeing to sex when she most emphatically did not feel like it!

'My behaviour isn't unique,' she countered quietly. 'Before we got engaged you wouldn't have dreamed of coming home and hurling accusations at me like that. You sounded like a bear with a sore head! No, worse!'

And she flounced out of the room before either of them had a chance to say anything else which they might later regret.

Her hands were shaking as she switched the gas off and took two plates out of the oven, where they were heating. She carried them through to the dining room, where she found Finn standing staring at the Christmas tree, its white candle lights reflected in the big glass windows which overlooked the park. There was a look of soft wonder in his eyes, some brief, faint glimpse of the innocent boy in the hard, handsome face of the man, and her heart turned over with love.

She put the plates down on the table. 'Do you like it?'

'You don't usually put it up quite so early,' he observed, his attention still caught by the bright glitter.

'I couldn't wait,' she prevaricated, vowing to tell him about the interview. Tomorrow. 'And you still haven't answered my question. Do you like it?'

He turned to face her, his eyes as darkly and as beautifully green as the fragrant pine. 'Sweetheart, I love it—it's the most beautiful tree I've ever seen!'

'You said that last year.'

'Did I?' he smiled.

'Yes! And the year before!'

'In fact, every Christmas we've spent together, even before we were officially a "couple",' he murmured, his eyes slowly travelling over her, looking at her properly for the first time since he had arrived home. 'And how many Christmases is that, Amber?'

'F-four,' she stumbled, because the way his eyes were searing over her was sending her pulses racing. 'Can't you remember?'

'I'm having a little difficulty with my thoughts just now,' he admitted deliberately.

Now she was ready to play the game. There was no danger of the flat burning down and, quite frankly, the sight of the chicken congealing in its coconut and coriander sauce was making her feel slightly queasy. She just wanted to lose herself in his arms and forget about the hurtful things they had said. And the lie she had told him...

'Are you?' she asked, her voice husky.

'Mmm.'

'Why's that?'

'Because you're distracting me, sweetheart, that's why. I can't seem to think of anything right now, except...' His voice tailed off as his pupils dilated in a look of desire that made Amber feel positively *brazen*.

'Except?'

'Come here,' he whispered.

Amber supposed that a more liberated woman than herself might have requested that *he* come to *her*. Because he was the one who had arrived home in such a foul temper.

She opened her mouth to say so, but something irresistibly compelling in the depths of those thick-lashed eyes made the words die hopelessly on her lips and she went straight into his arms.

He enfolded her in his embrace, rubbing his chin

against the silky softness of her hair, and she felt his body come alive against her. It had always been like that between them. That instant. That overwhelming. Sometimes she worried that the physical side was almost *too* good between them—because if that ever faded, then would there be enough left to sustain them?

'God—I want you, Amber,' he groaned.

'I'd n-never have guessed.' She swallowed down her excitement.

'So badly.'

She felt her pulse pick up speed. 'So what do you want to do about it?'

'This.' His forefinger skated over the golden silk towards the zip-fastening at the front, brushing carelessly against her breast on its travels, so that she sucked in a painful breath of agonised longing.

'Finn!' This as he unhurriedly began to slide the zip down, a smile playing at the corners of his mouth as it tugged with resistance over the luscious swell of her breasts.

'What?'

She briefly closed her eyes with helpless pleasure. 'I don't remember,' she murmured, her voice sounding slurred—almost drugged—heavy and sweet as honey. He had taught her this, had taught her everything she knew about lovemaking, and he was a grand master. She knew what pleasures lay ahead. For Finn had shown her that anticipation was everything, no matter how long the preliminaries took. He had taught her to indulge her senses—all of them. Shown her that a cup of coffee would taste all the more delicious if you savoured the aroma first.

He eased the zip down to past her navel, so that her breasts, straining exquisitely against the ivory-coloured lace of her bra, were exposed to his hot and hungry gaze.

'God, I'm glad you never reached the ideal height for modelling,' he said suddenly.

Amber's eyes snapped open. 'What an odd thing to say! Especially at a time like this! Why on earth not?'

'Because then, my beauty, you would have dieted all these succulent curves away and there would be no heavy mounds of silken breast for me to take in my mouth and suckle. No rounded belly on which to cushion my head—'

'Finn!' His words made her weak and dizzy with desire. She swayed like a sapling in the wind, and Finn had to catch her hips between his hands to support her.

'Steady, sweetheart,' he murmured appreciatively as he observed her instantaneous response to the things he was saying. 'Steady.'

Words failed her. How could she be steady when his hands had begun working their magic in the secret places and crevices of her body?

'Is this a new dress?' he wanted to know as he eased it over her shoulders and it pooled with a silken whisper to the floor, and she was left standing in the ivory lace bra and matching knickers and the milky-sheened stockings.

His question let a little unwelcome reality seep into her mind. She had bought it to wear on Christmas Day, and then, when the photographer from *Wow!* had turned up, it had seemed the perfect outfit to put on. Because it was a Christmassy colour and also because there was something about new clothes which made a woman feel extra-confident...

Maybe now was the time to tell him about the interview—but Amber didn't even give it a second thought, because by now Finn was ruthlessly rubbing at one of her nipples through the ivory lace, the pad of his thumb creating a soft, sweet sorcery that had her melting against him again. 'Yes, it's new,' she sighed helplessly against him. 'I bought it last week. D-do you like it?'

'I'm not sure,' he mused, as he eased a practised knee between her thighs and followed it with purposeful fingers. 'I think on balance it looks better off than on.'

Amber gave a little yelp of pleasure as he skimmed a moist path along the centre of her panties, and she couldn't have stopped her thighs from opening in mute invitation even if she had wanted to.

'Do you like that?' he queried unnecessarily.

She shook her head. Sometimes she resented him for this. For reducing her to such a boneless, shaking wreck within seconds of laying one seductive finger on her. 'Hate it,' she husked defiantly.

He gave a low laugh. 'Oh, do you?' He slid the panties down to mid-thigh, then stopped, and Amber realised that she had been doing a hell of a lot of taking and not much giving. She often felt shy about taking the lead. But that wasn't really surprising, not when she stopped to think about it. For Finn had been making love to beautiful women since he was eighteen, while she had only ever known him...

With trembling fingers she lightly flattened the palm of her hand against his black jeans, to touch and incite the great throbbing swell of him. Then she began to falteringly unbuckle his belt, wondering whether she would ever acquire his smooth undressing technique, and he gave another low laugh of pleasure.

'Oh, that's what I like about you, sweetheart,' he murmured, his voice sultry with pure elation. 'The way you tremble and gasp with shock and excitement whenever I lay a finger on you. The way you touch me with hands which are both scared and eager. The way your eyes widen with disbelief when I fill you right up with every inch of me. You're like a virgin every time we make love, Amber.'

'Am I?' For some reason his words fired her up with both rebellion and desire. Was she always such a predictable lover? Didn't his words imply that she was somehow in awe of him? Gazing on him in wonderment, as if finding it difficult to believe that the great Finn Fitzgerald should be making love to *her*, poor little Amber O'Neil, from the wrong side of town? 'But I'm *not* a virgin, am I, Finn? Because a virgin wouldn't touch you here. Like this.' And she boldly splayed her hand across the most elemental part of him and felt him buck beneath her.

'God, yes,' he breathed. 'Do that some more. Oh, God, *yes*, Amber!'

She jerked the zip of his jeans down, taking care not to catch it on the ridge of desire which was nudging so insistently against her hand. Then she pushed the heavy denim fabric to his knees and rolled down the black Lycra briefs to follow. He sprang free against her fingers, as proud and hard and taut and silken as she imagined it was possible for a man to be.

She encircled him possessively, running the tips of her fingers greedily against the satin shaft, and felt his body judder with pleasure. Then she let her thumb flick against him, slowly, deliberately and provocatively, until she felt bold enough to bend her head towards him. She felt a great tension seize him and he pushed her away and levered her back up to face him.

'No!' he growled.

'Why not? You know you like it.'

'Just no!' He read the question in her eyes. 'Sometimes that particular act can be too...too...'

'Too?'

'Intimate, I guess.' He gave the answer reluctantly.

She gestured to their dishevelled clothing. 'And this isn't?'

'You know what I mean, Amber.'

She nodded slowly. 'What? That tonight you don't want to feel particularly intimate?'

'Not really, no.' He looked at her assessingly. 'Tonight I feel mean. Mad. Bad...' He let the word trail off on a sexy promise. 'Does that bother you?'

Regret was eclipsed by a rapidly mounting excitement. 'Not in the way you think, no—but it *does* sound controlling.'

'Then let me be in control tonight, baby,' he cajoled softly, as he ran his fingertips possessively down over her throat. 'Just for tonight.'

'Aren't you always?' she mocked back.

But he silenced her words very effectively with first his mouth and then his fingers, pushing her to the carpet, her underclothes all in disarray as he lowered his weight on top of her.

Some of his urgency communicated itself to her and she found herself twisting beneath him, trailing an eager and exploratory hand over his hips to slither between his thighs.

'Oh, baby,' he murmured, his voice like rough silk against her ear. 'Turn around and bend over.'

Physically curbed by panties stretched tightly across her thighs, Amber found she was shaking so much with excitement that she could barely obey him, and so he assisted her, positioning her with hands which incited her even further.

She could not see him, but she could feel his hands moving with feather-light torment over her inner thighs, caressing them with lazy pleasure until she thought she might go mad. He pressed his lips against the smooth satin globes of her buttocks, kissing every inch of her bottom. And she moaned. Pleaded with him for release. Until at last she felt him reposition himself so that he was pushing against her. And when he finally thrust into her she actually lost her grip on reality for a moment. Stars danced before her eyes and her head dipped down like a heavy load.

He stilled for a moment while her body accommodated him. 'Like that?' he whispered, his own voice shaky as he felt the tightness of her.

She felt so full that she couldn't answer, but maybe her body communicated all that he needed to know, for he began to move very, very slowly—and it was as though he had pierced her heart with the very core of himself, and she gave a small cry of disbelief as she felt him deep within her.

Ripples began to build immediately—swiftly becoming waves, which picked her up and buffeted her, the sensations overpowering her totally and leaving her gasping with disbelief as her orgasm built, exploded and finally began to ebb away. And when at last she was able to focus her eyes, it was to see that her brand-new dress was now a crumpled heap of golden silk after being ground beneath his knees.

She heard the sound of Finn sucking in long, hard breaths, struggling to control his laboured breathing even as his own spasms began to still inside her.

But it was an undignified position to be in, a feeling made even more acute by their angry words of earlier, and Amber was glad when he withdrew from her, and gently slid her half-mast panties back up and over her bottom.

She turned to face him. 'Mean, mad and bad was right,' she observed wryly.

'Very bad?' he teased.

'Terribly.'

'Your face is all pink,' he noted as he pulled his jeans back up.

'And yours is white—'

'Well, I was doing all the work,' he teased.

'Finn! Don't be so disgusting!'

He picked her hand up and kissed the palm very tenderly. 'I wasn't being disgusting, sweetheart,' he murmured. 'Merely a little graphic.'

'My dress is ruined.' She glanced over at the tangled heap of gleaming golden fabric.

'It'll clean up,' he said easily, then gave a slight frown. 'It's a fancy kind of dress for a Wednesday evening, isn't it? We weren't expecting anyone, were we?'

Amber pursed her lips together. 'Hardly,' came her wry response. 'And even if we were, we're not exactly in a position to greet anybody, are we?'

He grinned. 'I refuse to comment on position, for fear of being accused of being disgusting again!'

Amber laughed and reached over for the silk dress. 'Do you think we'll ever get round to eating supper?'

He sent a glance over at the neglected dishes on the table which were now lukewarm. 'Would you be terribly offended if I said that I couldn't face eating a huge meal right now?'

'Not hungry?'

He gave a huge yawn. 'I'm bushed. Shall we take our wine and some potato crisps and go and watch TV in bed?'

It sounded heavenly. It had been ages since they had done something quite as simple and as decadent as holing themselves up in their bedroom! 'Wonderful idea,' said Amber fervently. 'I'll go and shower, and then I'll join you.'

His eyes glittered. 'I might join *you*,' he murmured. 'In the shower.'

But Amber shook her head. That experience on the carpet just now had wiped her out—mentally *and* physically—and besides, Finn looked in need of rest far more than making love again. 'Go to bed,' she said softly.

'It's that engagement ring syndrome again. Clearly, our sex life is to be rationed to once a night from now on, I can see,' he said, shaking his dark ruffled hair in dismay, but his eyes were smiling.

'Wanna bet?' she drawled, giggling as he playfully slapped her lace-clad bottom on her way to the bathroom.

The home-maker in her was too strong to provide simply potato crisps, so she made cheese sandwiches to accompany them. And a bowl of blueberries. And thick, creamy yoghurt made from goat's milk. That should build him up, she thought with satisfaction as she carried the tray into the bedroom, her hair still damp from the shower.

She found Finn fast asleep, just as he had found her earlier. He had put their wineglasses down on the bedside tables and the rest of the bottle in an ice-bucket on the floor.

She put the tray down noiselessly, in order not to wake him, but he stirred anyway and the black eyelashes flickered open. He gazed at her sleepily.

'Hi.' He smiled.

'Hi.' She smiled back. 'Go back to sleep if you want. Though…' She hesitated, not wanting to sound like his mother. Or his sister. Philomena had been more of a mother to him than a sister.

'Though what?' he asked.

'You really ought to eat more, Finn. It isn't good to skip meals, you know!'

He sat up and yawned, and then handed her a glass

of wine. 'So how's Ursula?' he enquired, as he took a sip.

Amber stared at him blankly. 'Ursula?'

Finn shot her a frowning look. 'Yes, Ursula. Your sister,' he elucidated, a deep seam of mockery running through his voice. 'You spent the afternoon with her, remember? You were drinking champagne with her. What's she been up to?'

Tell him, urged the voice of common sense. Just *tell* him about the interview.

I'll tell him tomorrow, Amber decided firmly.

'Not a lot.' She shrugged uneasily, and took a great big mouthful of wine.

CHAPTER THREE

THE office was crowded with models and gaudy paper-chains when Finn exploded into it like a dark starburst. Like some black-clad, avenging devil, he strode over to where Amber was sitting and hurled a magazine down onto the desk in front of her.

'Just what in God's name do you think you're up to, Amber?' he snarled, as angry as she had ever seen him.

It was all her chickens coming home to roost at the same time; all her nemeses arrived at once. And it served her right—she should have told him straight away. 'Finn—' she began placatingly.

'Don't you "Finn" me!' he ground out, as though he found the words intolerable to say. 'I want some kind of explanation as to why you saw fit to share our secrets with this tacky...' his mouth contorted with disdain as he gestured towards the brightly coloured photographs '...rubbish,' he snorted. 'And I want it now!'

If they had been alone she would have told him straight out what she had done—but they were not alone. They were surrounded by models of both sexes, all of them pale and gangling and, more importantly, all of them young. And for once they were looking vaguely interested in what was going on, instead of adopting their usual collective hangdog expression. Although usually their boss would not be waving his hands around as if he were conducting an orchestra.

And Amber was a kind of role model to those young people. She handed out more than bookings—she was pretty free with coffee and advice if they wanted her to be. She also listened patiently to their problems. If she let Finn snarl and speak to her in that derogatory fashion then surely she would be sending out the subliminal message that such arrogant behaviour was okay. And it wasn't okay.

She had sold a fairly innocuous story to a popular magazine, that was all—but from the way Finn was glowering at her anyone would think she had been involved in some bizarre sex act with the photographer!

'Finn—'

'I'm waiting, Amber,' he interrupted coldly.

That did it. She saw watching mouths fall open in wonder. 'Then you'll have a long wait,' she returned icily, saved, literally, by the bell, as the phone rang and she blithely began speaking into the mike attached to her headset.

She hoped that no one was noticing how much her hand was trembling as she tried to carry on the commonplace conversation as normal.

'You'd like to take out an option on CiCi Brown? For Wednesday afternoon?' She clicked CiCi's name up onto her computer screen and the model's weekly schedule appeared immediately. 'No, that's fine. She has a "go-see" in the morning, but that's only in Soho, so she'll get to you by midday with no problem.' Amber nodded and studiously avoided looking in Finn's direction. 'No. I understand. Great. Yeah. Sure. Bye.' She put the phone down. 'Finn, we'll have to have this conversation some other time.'

But he shook his head inexorably. 'Some other place, maybe. Perhaps you'd like to come into my office, Amber?'

She met the angry green stare. 'And if I refuse?'

His smile was bland and meaningless—and in that

loaded and uncomfortable moment he might have been a complete stranger.

'Then we'll be forced to entertain all these pretty young things—' he flashed a winning smile at the assembled throng '—with our little *spat*!' And he spat the word out, as if to illustrate his point.

Amber glowered at him. Wasn't that called blackmail? Would she be considered submissive if she succumbed to it? Because surely the bottom line was that she *did* feel guilty about not having plucked up courage to tell Finn about the interview—and at least if they were in the privacy of his office she would tell him so. Very sweetly.

She gave Debby, the other booker, a tight smile. 'Excuse me for a minute, Debby. I won't be long.'

Debby's answering look was disbelieving, but she nodded anyway, and the unusual silence continued as Amber picked up the magazine and trooped across the office, following Finn into the inner sanctum of his room.

As soon as they were inside he turned on her. 'Shut the door!' he snarled.

She was tempted to tell him to moderate his tone, but not for long. Instead, she slammed the door shut so loudly that it made him start, and then she sent a mutinous look searing across the office. 'There!' she flared. 'Go ahead and shout! If you want to make a big song and dance about it—I will, too!'

'Are you out of your tiny little *mind*?'

'To tie myself to a power-hungry megalomaniac like you, you mean?'

'To involve yourself in something like *that*—' He cast a withering glance at the magazine she was hugging in her arms, as though protecting it from his anger.

'Oh, for goodness' sake, Finn—stop overreacting! It's

a harmless little bit of gossip, that's all. I've hardly divulged your inside leg measurement to the waiting world!'

He gave her a measured look. 'Have you read it?'

Something in his eyes made her start to feel nervous. 'Well, no. Not yet. I've been working all morning and I haven't had a chance to—'

'Then why don't you take a look before you make judgements on it?' he interrupted silkily.

Something in his eyes was now making her feel very jumpy indeed. She began to open the magazine out while Finn went to stand over by the window, and the forbidding set of his broad shoulders was formidable as he stood silhouetted against the grey winter sky.

Amber blanched. She was on the cover of the magazine, for heaven's sake—the *cover*! Standing there in front of the Christmas tree in their flat, wearing the gleaming golden dress which afterwards had been discarded so ruthlessly, grinning into the camera and looking all twinkly-eyed and radiant. Her left hand was fiddling with the amber beads she wore at her neck, so that her diamond ring glittered like a trophy. Still, it wasn't *that* bad. And, although he didn't like references to his former career, the banner headline simply read: 'WHY LIFE WITH MODEL-MAN FINN IS SO ENGAGING!'

Amber cleared her throat and addressed 'model-man' Finn's back. 'Must be an arid time for news if we've made the front cover!' she joked blithely, and then, in a laughable attempt to lighten the mood, added, 'Our Christmas tree looks nice, doesn't it?'

'Why don't you take a look inside?' he suggested, in a voice so bland it spooked her.

Amber examined the magazine's index and quickly turned to page forty. And shuddered. Oh, Lord—*why* had she done it?

At the time, reclining against the cushions on their bed wearing a black evening dress had seemed like a bit of fun—but the photographic reality made her cringe. She looked like an overblown strumpet—her breasts pushing forward against the shiny material like two pendulous melons. But that wasn't the worst of it. Just what did the journalist think he was playing at? How *dared* he entitle the piece 'BATHROOM PROPOSAL FROM ADVENTUROUS LOVER!'?

Amber let her eyes scan the text. It was stomach-churningly bad, and that was being kind about it. Somehow, the journalist had managed to distort everything she had said so that the whole story made *her* sound like a cross between Cinderella and a hooker, while Finn came across as some seducer of innocent young employees!

'Oh, my God,' she said weakly, and flopped down into the chair, wincing at another Christmas tree shot, in which she looked completely brainless.

'Have you got to the bit where it tells the readers to...' Finn put on a bitingly cruel voice as he snatched the magazine from her to read, '''Prepare yourself for the Wedding of the Year, when Finn guides the lovely Amber up the aisle on St Valentine's Day...''' He turned angry green eyes on her as he spread the magazine over his desk, his fingers recoiling from the glossy pages as if they were contaminated. 'A Valentine's Day wedding?' he demanded. '*Really?* It's news to me, sugar!'

'But you *did* mention that we might get married on Valentine's Day, Finn!' she protested. 'You know you did!'

'I also once suggested that you might like to lightly scrape your fingernails over my buttocks,' he bit back coldly. 'But I would hope you wouldn't tell *that* to a national magazine! Although judging by your other in-discretions—' His eyes blazed furious green fire as he stared at her, as if he was seeing an entirely new side to her, a side he didn't like very much at all. 'Did you tell them I made love to you in the bathroom before pro-posing?'

'Of *course* I didn't!'

'There's no "of course" about it!' he stormed, jab-bing at a paragraph with his finger. 'That is what is very strongly implied in this piece. And it's sordid.'

She read the paragraph he was indicating and cringed. He was right—that particular part of the article *was* rather sordid.

'And as for telling them word for word how we met—' He slowly shook his dark head in disbelief, as though her actions were inexplicable to him.

Amber had had enough. 'And is that such a heinous crime?' she demanded. 'You don't work for the Secret Service, you know, Finn! What's wrong with telling them about an innocent little love story?'

'My private life is supposed to be just that,' he gritted back. *'Private!'*

'Yes,' she answered flatly. 'So it would seem. I'll re-member that in future.'

But an odd, fractured kind of silence greeted her words, broken only by the glugging of the coffee ma-chine in the corner, and Amber's heart suddenly froze as she looked into his face and realised just how angry he was.

The mention of the word 'future' had produced an icy atmosphere—but surely she hadn't blown the whole re-lationship on the strength of one stupid article?

His face was grim as his green eyes scoured her face, as if looking for clues to why she had done it. 'And did you have to describe me quite so crudely?' he demanded.

'I—'

'"Testosterone personified",' he quoted in disgust. 'I was disappointed, Amber—I thought that *you* of all people had looked at the man beneath, and not just the wrapping!'

'They put words into my mouth!' she defended. 'That's what journalists do, Finn—*you* know that!'

'Precisely!' he snapped. 'Which is why I don't give interviews. And if you knew that—then you shouldn't have done either!'

'Oh, change the record!'

'You know that I work in a high-profile industry—and that's one reason why I guard my privacy so jealously.' His eyes were glacial now—cold and clear and questioning. 'I can't figure out what made you do it, that's all. Maybe if I could, I might feel a little less angry about it. So why, Amber? Just tell me that.'

She was quiet for a moment, knowing how important it was that he understood her motives. 'Because I wanted to make our engagement feel real, I guess.'

'I don't understand.'

Well, neither did she, and that was half the trouble. Amber stared at him helplessly, realising that it was better to risk looking a fool and to tell him the truth... anything to banish that cold, hard and unfamiliar look in his eyes. 'It's just that the engagement seemed like a one-off production—something that had nothing to do with *our* lives.'

'I don't understand,' he said again.

'I'm *trying* to explain!' she told him frustratedly. 'We got engaged after that party—'

'In the *bathroom*,' he bit out. 'As the whole world now knows.'

'Not the *whole* world!' she corrected pithily. 'Just the readers of *Wow!* magazine.' She heaved out a great sigh. 'You bought the ring and surprised me and it was wonderful, and then…then…' her voice trembled momentarily '…*nothing*.' She shrugged her shoulders. 'You were the one who had wanted to make this great big wonderfully romantic gesture, but afterwards you seemed to act like it had never happened.'

Finn knitted his dark brows together. 'How?'

'Well, you never talked about marriage, or wedding plans. We never had the usual type of conversations that people have when they have just committed to each other like that.'

'Such as?'

'Um…' Amber realised that she was blushing '…babies, I suppose—'

'Babies?' Finn looked at her in surprise. 'You mean you want to have a baby?'

'Of course I don't want to have a baby! Well, I do. But not yet! But I assumed that we would both want them some time in the future—that's if we're lucky enough to be able to have them.'

Finn perched on the edge of his desk, his black-denimed legs spread out in front of him as he observed her thoughtfully. 'But we didn't discuss it?'

Amber shook her head. 'No. Or where we would live. In fact, we don't seem to have talked about anything very much for ages. You're so busy all the time that sometimes I feel I hardly see you. It was as though the whole engagement thing had never happened—the only reality was the diamond, and after a while I stopped noticing even that.'

His eyebrows lifted up, disappearing briefly into the thickness of his dark, ruffled hair. 'And wouldn't it have been simpler to have just sat down and talked about what was bothering you, Amber? Rather than broadcasting it to the world like this?'

'When?' she shot back. 'You always seem so tied up these days. Working all the hours that God sends. Spending hours on the phone to *Birgitta*, as you seem to like to do so much,' she emphasised, even as she despised herself for her unreasonable jealousy.

'We're not back onto *that*, are we?' he questioned wearily.

She ignored the content of his question and concentrated instead on the way he had expressed it. He sounded exhausted—but her question came out sounding querulous instead of concerned. 'Tell me, have you taken a good look at yourself in the mirror just lately, Finn? You look absolutely wiped out.'

His eyes narrowed. 'I leave vanity to the models,' he told her drawlingly. 'That's one of the reasons I gave up doing it for a living.'

'Is it?' Amber met his eyes. 'Maybe you gave up modelling because you couldn't stand taking orders from other people!' she observed slowly. 'You make the decisions because you always know best, Finn—or rather you think you do!'

'Do I?'

'Sure you do.'

He fixed her with a steady look. 'So how come you've never told me this before?'

'Maybe there was no need to when our relationship was in its first lovey-dovey stages—'

'But it's not any more? Is that what you mean?'

'Perhaps some of the gloss has worn thin and I'm scratching beneath the surface.' She lifted her chin. 'And discovering that I don't much like what I find.'

His gaze didn't waver. 'This is fast escalating into a

demonstration of major differences between us, Amber,' he said. 'Don't you think?'

And then she knew real fear. Fear of having pushed him that fraction too far. Because, sitting poised so elegantly and so nonchalantly on his desk, Finn also looked frighteningly *distant*. Distant enough to *end* the relationship? she wondered.

Eager to kiss and make up, she held out her hand towards him, but he didn't take it, just looked at her questioningly.

'What?'

'Please.' It came out all wrong; she hadn't meant to plead with him.

He shook his head. 'I'm not going to make love to you, Amber, not now and not here. I have work to do and I'm still angry.'

She bit back her own furious response that everything always had to be on *his* terms, that they could only ever make love at inappropriate times if *Finn* wished it. 'Oh, don't worry, Finn,' she told him proudly. 'I haven't been reduced to begging you to make love to me. I just want you to come over to the mirror and take a look at yourself.'

He didn't take her hand, but something in her eyes made him follow her over to the looking-glass, which was both large and cruelly accurate. The room was used for casting sessions. Clients would sit and watch while model after model streamed into the room, hoping to be chosen for the job. The mirror was designed to reflect every tiny detail, every pound gained, every wrinkle highlighted—and nothing could escape its brutally faithful eye.

The two of them stood motionless in front of their reflections, until Finn met Amber's troubled blue eyes with a question. 'So?' he queried.

Amber screwed up her face in confusion. Was he blind? Or did he simply not want to see what was as clear as day to her? 'Can't you see how pale you look, Finn? And how tired? Or am I just imagining those dark shadows underneath your eyes?'

'It's almost Christmas, Amber,' he told her, in a voice which was suddenly gentle. 'Things are much madder than usual. And Jackson is away.'

The gentle tone was her undoing, and Amber felt her mouth trembling so precariously that she had to bite her lips to stop it. In a minute she would start blubbing— and that would be the second time recently that it had happened. Much more and it would be starting to be a habit. 'Yes, I know they are,' she replied hollowly.

He sighed, and then put his arms around her and rested his head on hers.

She tried to shake him off. 'Don't!'

'Don't you like me touching you?'

Her eyes were like dark sapphire stars. 'Don't be so bloody *arrogant*, Finn! You know darned well that I like you touching me—what I *don't* like is arguing and sniping and that's all we seem to have done just lately.'

He let her go. 'It'll get better after Christmas when Jackson gets back,' he promised. 'Lots of quiet nights in—just the two of us.' He brushed a lock of golden hair from her cheek and gave her his most irresistible smile, which almost countered the rueful expression in his eyes, and Amber wondered what was coming next. She didn't have to wait long to find out.

'But not yet,' he murmured. 'You haven't forgotten that it's the Prodigy party tonight? Remember? I said we'd pop in.'

Actually, she *had* forgotten, but maybe that wasn't so surprising, since all her time seemed to have been taken up with worrying about the state of their relationship just lately.

Prodigy was one of the biggest perfume and make-up manufacturers in the business. Major big time, in fact. And their parties were legendary. Finn and Jackson's agency had supplied them with Prodigy's last two 'Faces', including their current one—the scrumptious and fragile-looking Karolina Lindberg, who was about to be launched on the inside pages of every glossy over the globe.

Amber looked at Finn worriedly. 'But my sister is coming round for supper.'

'Can't you cancel?'

'No, I *can't* cancel—quite apart from the fact that she's been away for a couple of weeks, you know that Ursula doesn't get many evenings out.'

'That's hardly our fault, is it, Amber?'

She gave him a long, considering look, and in that moment felt angrier than she could ever have imagined feeling towards the man she had once thought could do no wrong. 'I can't believe you just said that,' she told him quietly.

He leaned towards her. 'Why not, when it's the truth? Your sister has carved out a certain kind of life for herself. She doesn't go out on dates—well, that's up to her, isn't it? It's her choice, no one else's. And if she chooses to carry a torch for a man who is patently unobtainable, then that too is her choice—'

'She is *not* carrying a torch for Ross Sheridan!' contradicted Amber heatedly.

Finn smiled triumphantly. 'Oh, really?' came his soft rebuttal. 'Strange that you knew straight away who I was talking about!'

'Ross is her boss—'

'I was *your* boss,' he pointed out.

'But he's *married*!'

'Ah.' Finn's eyes became guarded. *'Married!'*

'Yes, *married*!'

He shrugged. 'But a gold band never stopped people having extra-marital liaisons, did it? As the history books have shown us time and time again—'

'Oh, please, don't be so cynical! Or so patronising! My sister would *not* mess around with a married man!' she told him, so fiercely that he held his hand up.

'Maybe she wouldn't,' he conceded. 'And I certainly didn't mean to cast doubts on her morality. But I'm not going to feel sorry for her, Amber, and neither will I pity her simply because she seems hell-bent on spending the rest of her life in isolation.'

Which still hadn't solved what to do about tonight. 'Well, she isn't planning to spend *tonight* in isolation—she's coming round for supper with us. So what will I do about the Prodigy party?'

'Why don't you bring Ursula along with us?'

'Really?'

He shrugged. 'Why not?'

'Won't they mind?'

'Of course they won't mind! And who knows? She might meet someone—though of course she could meet a Mr Universe, with brains and a fortune to boot, and she'd still find something wrong with him by virtue of the fact that he wasn't Ross Sheridan.'

Amber fixed him with a curious look. 'You aren't jealous of Ross Sheridan, by any chance?'

Finn raised his eyebrows and smiled the kind of disbelieving smile which told Amber that he had never felt jealous of another man in his life. 'Of course not. I like Ross. I just think that both he and your sister are miserable—and if they're not going to get it together then maybe she should stop working for him.'

Amber thought that Finn was very good at discussing other people's problems rather than his own. But then maybe, unlike Amber, he just hadn't come around to realising that they actually *had* a problem. Because if a couple got engaged and then spent a big chunk of their time bitching at one other, then surely that didn't bode well for their long-term future, did it?

'Okay,' she agreed, glad to have something else to think about. 'I'll ring Ursula and ask her.'

CHAPTER FOUR

IT WAS early evening when the front doorbell pealed out over the flat. Amber pressed the clip into the back of her earring and cast a final glance at herself in the mirror. A dark blue silk dress which matched her eyes, golden hair gleaming to her shoulders and Finn's birthday sapphires in her ears. She looked sleek and expensive and very groomed, which was surprising in itself when she considered what she had been up to until a very short time ago.

'That'll be Ursula.' She glanced over towards the rumpled sheets of the bed, where Finn was still sprawled—all honeyed flesh and strong, long limbs against the white linen. Her heart did its habitual contraction. 'Are you getting up, Finn?'

She saw his green eyes dance wickedly and shook her head with a smile, thinking that there was nothing like sex to put Finn Fitzgerald in a good mood. 'And, no, that wasn't an invitation! Merely an observation that if you don't move that delectable body of yours out of bed pretty quick—then the party will be over before we get there.'

'Who cares?' he murmured sleepily.

'I thought you did. You were the one who wanted to go to the Prodigy party—and I telephoned Ursula to tell her to dress up specially. I think she's quite looking forward to it.' Amber cast a last look at her pink-flushed cheeks in the mirror. 'Just hurry up, Finn,' she pleaded. 'Ursula's at the door and I don't want her to think we've just had sex—'

'But we *have* just had sex,' he protested as he sat up and stretched his arms above his tousled head, the picture of sleepy contentment. 'That's what couples who live together generally do, sweetheart. We're not breaking any laws, you know.'

'I just think it's awkward for a single woman to have it thrown in her face—makes her feel out of it,' said Amber tartly, wondering, not for the first time, whether her sister was still a virgin. 'So hurry up, will you, Finn? I'll give her a drink while we're waiting.' And she shut the bedroom door firmly behind her.

Ursula was waiting patiently on the doorstep, and the two women kissed with the close affection of sisters who had endured a tough childhood and come through it relatively unscathed. Ursula lived on the other side of London and they tried to see as much of each other as they could—though Amber's relationship with Finn had inevitably conflicted with this and their meetings were far less frequent these days. She just wished that Ursula could find a man of her own to love.

'You look wonderful!' Amber smiled, thinking that the well-cut black silk dress made her sister look extremely elegant. 'Good holiday, was it?'

Ursula hesitated. 'It was…interesting. I'll tell you all about it in a minute.'

'Come on,' said Amber. 'Let's have some champagne. It *is* nearly Christmas, after all!'

Ursula looked over Amber's shoulder. 'Where's Finn?'

'He's just getting changed.'

Ursula nodded absently and followed Amber into the kitchen, where she was reaching into the fridge for a bottle. 'Don't open champagne just for me, will you, Amber?'

'No, I'm opening it for me, too!' laughed her sister

as she eased the cork out of the bottle with an explosive pop. 'What's up? Are you forswearing all booze?'

Ursula shook her head. 'I've been trying to lose weight for Christmas.'

'Well, you look—' Amber started to say, but Ursula interrupted her with a philosophical shrug.

'No, don't! Don't say whatever it was you were going to say! I look as plump as a currant bun,' Ursula said, with a stoicism she had acquired over the years. 'And that's the truth.'

'You're too hard on yourself,' protested Amber, thinking how well the black silk looked as it undulated down over her sister's generous curves.

Physically, at least, the two sisters could not have been more different. Amber's looks were head-turningly unusual—with her thick, glossy hair whose colour was almost impossible to define. Finn had once told her that it looked like golden syrup poured straight from the tin, but it had also been called ginger and Titian and even strawberry blonde. Her skin was pale, with golden freckles spattered onto a cute stub of a nose, and her mouth was full enough to be described as sultry. Apparently, she was the image of one of her great-aunts on her father's side, whereas Ursula took after their mother and looked as Irish as could be—with her thick, black hair and the soft roses which bloomed in her cheeks.

Ursula's deep blue eyes and the long, sweeping dark lashes were the same as Amber's, but all similarity stopped there. Amber had the kind of figure that most women would die for—leggy, narrow-hipped and slim-waisted, with lush breasts which seemed to defy gravity—while Ursula was unfashionably buxom. She often wished that she had lived in another age, when creamy flesh and cushioned shoulders and hips were seen as highly desirable and attractive. But she did not. Instead, she inhabited a world which had elevated thinness to an art form.

She gave Amber a fond smile. 'Perhaps if I didn't have a little sister who was a top model then it wouldn't make so much difference what my figure looked like!'

'But I'm not a top model!' objected Amber as she poured them each a tall glass of champagne. 'I've just done bits of work here and there, because I'm not quite tall enough—'

'And because Finn likes you where he can see you,' put in Ursula wryly.

Amber sat opposite her sister. 'Are you saying that Finn is possessive?'

Ursula glanced over at the Christmas tree. 'I'm saying that he's territorial. What's his is his, and no one else's—I guess that's what comes of being the youngest of seven children. Though I have to admit I was surprised that he let you do that piece in *Wow!* magazine.'

Amber nearly choked on her drink. 'You've seen it?'

Ursula threw her a questioning look. 'Oh, Amber!' she exclaimed. 'Who *hasn't* seen it? It's on every newsstand in the country.'

'What did you think of it?'

Ursula screwed her face up. 'Not a lot, if you want the truth. Oh, I didn't dislike it or anything—it just seemed rather...*silly*, that's all. Unnecessary.' She looked over at her sister curiously. 'Did Finn really make love to you in the bathroom before he proposed?'

'But I didn't *say* that!' Amber yelped indignantly.

'Well, either you implied it, or the journalist is good at concocting fairy tales,' came Ursula's dry response. 'If it's the former then I suspect you're in big trouble with Finn, and if it's the latter—' and her eyes sparkled with mischief '—then it seems to me that you have a good case for litigation.'

Amber closed her eyes. 'Don't! Finn's absolutely furious.'

'I'm not surprised! What in the name of God possessed you to do it?'

Amber shook her head. It would be selfish to tell her sister that her actions had been motivated by feelings of insecurity. What patience would Ursula have if she came out with a statement like that? When she had a lovely home, a job she enjoyed and Finn's ring on her finger—what on earth was there to be insecure about? 'Brainstorm,' she said evasively.

'Which of you is having one?' came a deep velvet voice as Finn came into the room, looking, thought Amber hungrily, good enough to eat, in his dark dinner suit and whiter-than-white shirt.

'Hello, Ursula,' he said, and bent to kiss her on the cheek.

'Hi, Finn.' Ursula smiled up at him. 'Amber was the one having the brainstorm—when she did that terrible interview for *Wow!*'

Finn didn't react at all; not a flicker of emotion crossed his face as he helped himself to a glass of soda. 'Well, that's the very *last* interview she's doing, isn't it, sweetheart?'

Behind her fixed smile, Amber gritted her teeth. It was one thing deciding for yourself that you didn't want to do something—but quite another altogether for someone else to tell you not to in that polite, but very controlling way! Still... 'Absolutely the last.' She nodded obediently.

Finn sat on the arm of one of the chairs and turned to Ursula. 'So how's work?'

'Fine.'

'And Ross?'

Ursula didn't miss a beat. 'He's fine.'

'And the wonderful world of advertising?'

'Would you believe that's fine, too?' said Ursula lightly, sending Amber a wordless plea.

Amber shot a warning glance in Finn's direction before smoothly changing the subject. 'And you don't mind coming to this party for an hour or two, do you? They've signed up one of our newest models, so it's a bit of a duty visit.'

Ursula shook her head. 'I don't mind at all—I don't go out enough, I know that. Everyone tells me often enough! But it's great to get the chance to talk before we go because, actually, I've had some very exciting news.'

In view of what she and Finn had been discussing earlier, and seeing the sparkle in her sister's deep blue eyes, Amber jumped to entirely the wrong conclusion. 'Don't tell me that Ross is getting a divorce?'

A pin-drop silence followed this remark, and Amber was just about to stumble her apologies when Ursula cleared her throat, desperate to change the subject and glad that she had a legitimate reason for doing so.

'Not that he's told me!' she joked bravely. 'No, my news is far more exciting than that!'

'Then tell,' murmured Finn.

'Well, you know that you and Amber are having a Valentine's Day wedding?' Ursula began, but something in Amber's face made her falter. 'Y-you *are*, aren't you?'

'Apparently,' said Finn tonelessly. 'Did you read that in *Wow!*? Or maybe in *another* publication I've yet to hear about?'

Ursula ignored Amber's beseeching look, quickly realising from the atmosphere that she was treading on eggshells. Whatever she said was bound to be the wrong thing, so maybe it was best if she simply told the truth.

'Well, I *did* read it there, yes, Finn—and I've already told Amber that I thought it was a foolish and ill-advised article.'

Finn nodded, narrow-eyed and wary. 'Thank God that *someone* in the family can see sense!'

'But Amber had already told me about the Valentine date—she said you'd mentioned it once. Anyway, you're going to have to change it. Which is why I've brought you *this*!' She smiled as she fumbled around in her over-size handbag and withdrew a crumpled-up article cut from a newspaper. She smoothed it out and spread it on the space on the sofa next to her, and both Amber and Finn leaned over to look at it with interest.

'It's a wedding dress,' said Finn slowly as he looked down at the picture of a full-length dress cut from ivory duchessne satin. It was a stark and yet subdued gown— the simplicity of the design softened by the buttery texture of the luxurious fabric. Finn had an eye for beauty which was not easily satisfied, but it was satisfied now. 'It's absolutely exquisite,' he murmured appreciatively, and looked at Ursula with a question in his eyes.

'Yes,' agreed Ursula, but her eyes were fixed unwaveringly on her sister. 'It is.'

Amber had gone as white as a snowdrop. It was several moments before she could speak. 'Mother's dress,' she breathed in disbelief. 'It's Mother's dress!'

Ursula thought that her sister might faint away, she looked so pale. She shook her head. 'No, it isn't. I know it looks like it, but it isn't. It's a *copy* of Mother's dress,' she explained quickly. 'Not the real thing—but as close as you can get.'

Finn frowned with concern as he took Amber's hand. 'Are you okay, sweetheart?'

She gripped his hand tightly, needing the warmth and the reassurance and wishing that she could freeze-frame the comfort and the closeness that his touch inspired at that moment. 'Y-yes, I'm okay,' she said shakily.

'Then would someone mind telling me what is going on?' asked Finn. 'What's the significance behind this particular wedding dress?'

Ursula nodded and sought to condense the story into its most tellable form, since Amber had obviously said nothing to him about the dress. 'Years and years ago, our mother worked as a cleaner in a big department store in Knightsbridge—did you know that?'

He nodded. 'Vaguely. I think Amber mentioned it when we first met.'

'Well, in the store there was a beautiful designer-made wedding dress and Mum absolutely fell in love with it. She used to go and look at it whenever she got a spare moment. And she couldn't believe it when no one wanted it and it was drastically reduced in the sales. So she queued up all night and bought it herself.'

'But why?' queried Finn. 'Wasn't she married at the time?'

'She was. She did it because she was a complete romantic,' said Amber softly. 'Despite her circumstances.'

'Go on,' said Finn, his interest alight.

Ursula took up the story again. 'It was to be *our* wedding dress—mine and Amber's—to wear when *we* got married; that's why she bought it. We used to touch it through the plastic covering and imagine ourselves wearing it...' Her voice faltered. 'Then our father died and we had no money, and so Mother had to sell the dress, even though it broke her heart to do so.'

'And where is it now?'

'No one knows. A man called Luke Goodwin is trying to find it—but that's another story. But the daughter of the original designer has made a dress that's very similar—and that's this one.' She jabbed at the photo with one well-upholstered finger. 'She's just opened a wedding dress shop out near Winchester, and she's raffling *this* dress—the copy—as a prize. And I've entered your name in the competition, Amber!'

Amber was trying to take it all in, but her most overriding thought was that it seemed somehow *inappropriate* to be talking about weddings when she and Finn had been arguing so much lately. Instead she tugged down the gleaming sapphire silk of the dress she was wearing and bit her lip. 'I shouldn't think I stand much chance of winning it, do you?'

Ursula put down her empty glass, her eyes shining with excitement. 'No, you don't—but that doesn't *matter*!'

Amber blinked. 'I'm not sure I follow what you're saying.'

'The girl who designed *this* dress—her name is Holly Lovelace and you'd really like her—she designs wedding dresses for a living. And if you don't win *this* one, then she says that she'll make a copy of it for you. Made to measure—it'll be perfect—and just like Mother's! It would take a keen eye to be able to tell the difference between the two gowns. The only snag is you can't have it till March. The bridal magazine sponsoring the competition are doing a big feature on it then, and they don't want it to be worn before.' Ursula swallowed down her emotion. 'Just think, Amber—delay the wedding for a month and Mother's dream could come true in spite of everything! You could end up wearing a dress exactly like the one she had always wanted you to wear!'

Amber was silent for a moment. The sight of the wedding dress had brought memories of her childhood back in sharp focus. She remembered the dark and poky flat—the stifling claustrophobia of the winter months as the rain had trickled in relentless grey sheets down the panes of glass, the condensation turning the room into a green-house.

Then, the beautiful and costly wedding dress had represented another world. A world where clothes were carefully made and bought for reasons other than being cheap and warm. A world where civilised meals were eaten off fine china instead of chipped and mismatched seconds. A world where brides drifted down aisles clothed in the finest silks and satins instead of sheepishly sneaking into the nearest register office, with their Sunday best concealing the early stages of pregnancy.

But then, as now, the dress had seemed curiously out of place. Amber did not want to discuss the possibility of a wedding—on Valentine's Day or any other time. It seemed that she was jumping the gun by miles, and she certainly did not want Finn to feel he was being pushed into anything he didn't want to do.

'What do you think?' Ursula's voice seemed to come from a long way away.

Amber looked up blankly, meeting Finn's keen green gaze which cut through her emotional armour like a sword. She wanted the wedding dress to *mean* something right then—hell, it *did* mean something, because it reminded her of her mother. But the story had been tainted by the disquieting inner knowledge that all was not right between her and Finn.

Did he sense something of her disillusion? Was that why his thumb began to almost absently stroke the back of her hand in a way she was sure was designed to be comforting, but—because it was Finn—made her feel almost bereft with longing? So that she would have thrown herself into his arms and begged him to kiss her and make everything all right with that kiss, as he had always managed to do in the past.

But she could not do that. And not just because she

had an audience in Ursula, either. Amber realised that to keep losing herself in some kind of sensual thrall to Finn was a bit like burying her head in the sand. Sex was supposed to *add* something to a relationship—not just blot out the bits you found too uncomfortable to confront.

Watching closely for his reaction, Amber kept her gaze firmly fixed on Finn's face. 'Do *you* like the wedding dress, Finn?'

'I'm sure that you'd look absolutely beautiful in it, Amber.'

Her gaze didn't waver, but she thought that, as answers went, his was smooth and bland. And utterly noncommittal.

'So shall I leave you Holly's phone number?' asked Ursula eagerly.

'Yes, do. Thanks,' said Amber as Ursula handed her an ivory card embossed with gold and bearing the message: 'Lovelace Brides: wedding gowns to fall in love with!', followed by a Hampshire telephone number.

'And you *will* contact her, won't you, Amber?' asked Ursula.

Amber attempted to use a noncommittal smile very similar to the one Finn had just flashed at her. It was easy if you tried hard enough. 'We'll see,' she prevaricated. She put her empty glass down on the table. 'Gosh! All that champagne has made me feel quite light-headed! I need some food to act as blotting paper! What time are we due at the Prodigy party, Finn?'

He looked at his wristwatch and frowned, but then he had been frowning for the best part of a minute anyway, thought Amber.

'About half an hour ago,' he said shortly. 'Come on, ladies—it's time to go!'

* * *

Prodigy might have been expected to have taken over a suite at the Granchester Hotel—a venue which was inevitably used for hyped-up events which were brash and loud and 'happening'. Events where money was no object other than to be poured down people's throats in the form of the finest bubbly, and where newspaper and magazine photographers had been given prime spots from which to capture the best pictures of the rich and famous for the next morning's papers.

However, on this occasion they had elected to use the private function room of one of the capital's newest and trendiest restaurants—*Caveat Emptor!* The private room could only accommodate one hundred guests, and consequently the tickets were like gold-dust.

Without the two security guards to clear their path outside, it would have been like fighting their way to the front of the crowd at a football match.

As soon as he had seen them safely into the sanctum of the restaurant, Finn disappeared to find the head of Prodigy. 'I'd better just okay it with him about having brought Ursula,' he murmured, and swiftly dropped a kiss on the top of Amber's gleaming head. 'And then I'll check out that Karolina is behaving herself. Okay?'

'Okay,' nodded Amber.

The two sisters went off in search of the powder room, and Amber was just leaning towards the mirror to touch up her lipstick when she caught Ursula's reflection staring at her curiously in the mirror.

'Everything *is* okay, isn't it, Amber?'

Amber kept her face poker-straight as she blotted off the excess lipstick with a tissue. 'In what way?'

Ursula shifted uncomfortably, her face growing pink. 'I don't know…you seem…*different*, somehow. Sort of preoccupied. And tense, too. So does Finn. Is there something going on that I should know about?'

Amber shook her head, the fall of syrup-gold hair swaying like heavy silk around her neck. 'Nothing's going on. I'm tired, but Finn is even more tired. He's been working too hard in the run-up to Christmas, and Jackson's away. Plus he's mad with me for doing the interview. That's all.'

'Okay.' Ursula hesitated. 'If something was wrong—you *would* tell me, wouldn't you?'

Amber laughed. 'Of course I would! Who else would I tell? I'm closer to you than to anyone!'

Gratified, Ursula smiled into the mirror at her sister and wondered whether to put any lipstick on, but decided against it. After all, no one would be looking at *her* tonight! Not with Amber standing beside her.

'Come on.' Amber took Ursula's arm and squeezed it affectionately. 'He'll be even madder if we keep him waiting!'

They walked into the sumptuous Silver Room, where they caught a glimpse of Karolina Lindberg, surrounded by a sea of photographers. Amber looked around for Finn. He was taller than most of the men there, and she spotted his dark head as soon as he entered the room. So did some of the other women, judging by the speed at which several heads swivelled round. His eyes searched them out and he came over to where they stood.

'They've certainly gone to town on the decor,' he observed drily. 'What do you think?'

'Eye-catching,' murmured Amber, as a silver-clad waitress wiggled by, and he smiled.

Ursula was busy looking around her, taking in the silver satin tablecloths which gleamed like starlight. The candles were silver and so were the goblets, and silver stars were pinned onto swathes of black netting which were draped artistically from the ceiling. 'I'm *terribly* impressed!'

Finn narrowed his eyes. 'But you work in advertising, too, Ursula—you must come to functions like this all the time.'

'No.' Ursula shook her head. 'I tend not to.' She had made that a ground rule right from the word go—to attend as few functions as she could. It made it easier to handle her feelings for her boss that way. Functions meant free-flowing wine and the relaxations of barriers erected at work, and when they involved a man you were trying desperately hard not to love they were best avoided. She tried to catch a better look at Karolina through the mêlée of photographers who surrounded her. 'Your model is popular,' she observed drily. 'They're like bees round a honey-pot!'

Karolina was clearly enjoying herself hugely, draped all over a white satin sofa—all six feet of her. She was wearing a pure white satin dress, with a garland of wild white roses crowning the moon-white tumble of her hair.

Ursula's mouth fell open as they moved closer. 'Heck—but she's absolutely *exquisite*!' she breathed.

'Isn't she?' agreed Finn, an unmistakable note of pride in his voice.

'And where did you find her?'

'Oh, Finn spotted her,' said Amber with a slow smile of recollection. 'Standing at Waterloo station wearing a pair of tatty old jeans and a windcheater. Her hair was crammed underneath a woolly hat and she didn't have a scrap of make-up on her face.'

'She must have looked very different,' Ursula observed.

Finn nodded. 'Uh-huh—but her bone structure was faultless and I knew she would photograph well. She had that indefinable something and I just knew she would go straight to the top.'

'So what do you do in that kind of situation?' asked Ursula curiously. 'Just go up to her and say, "I think you'd make a wonderful model—here's my card!"?'

'Something like that,' said Amber. 'In this business you're always on scout duty—looking for new talent. I am. Everyone at Allure is. That's the way this business works.'

'But don't you get funny looks when you approach total strangers at railway stations?' asked Ursula. 'Particularly if they're that young?'

'Finn never gets funny looks,' said Amber truthfully. 'Just hungry looks!'

'I don't do very much scouting these days,' said Finn. 'I tend to be more tied up in the office—and the day I saw Karolina, Amber was with me, which was nice.'

'So how do they know that you're not some evil abductor?'

'Does Finn *look* like your average abductor?' giggled Amber. 'They'd take one look at him and say, "Yes, *please*!"'

Finn smiled. 'If they're with a parent, or a friend—then so much the better,' he said. 'There's safety in numbers. Karolina happened to have her mother with her. But they can check out the business card before they contact me—just to reassure themselves that we're completely legit. And it isn't only girls we're after—we approach boys, too.'

Ursula watched in fascination as Karolina tossed her head back in a gesture designed to show off every inch of her firm and delectable body. 'How old is she?'

'She's sixteen.'

'So young,' observed Ursula.

'Yes,' Finn agreed softly. 'Some people say it's *too* young.'

Amber glanced up at him, at the way his profile had suddenly hardened. There had been no criticism in her sister's remark, and yet Amber still found herself springing to defend Finn's last statement.

'It *does* seem very young, doesn't it? But she still gets plenty of time for homework, and she's always chaperoned to make sure that unreasonable requests aren't made of her.'

At that moment Karolina spotted them, or, to be more precise, she spotted Finn. Waving her hand nonchalantly to disperse the clustering photographers, she rose fluidly to her feet and tottered towards them, on heels which were much too high. Though Amber noticed that Finn still towered over the young model.

'Finn!' Karolina exclaimed, with an instinctive and very sexy little curving smile which added about a decade to her real age. 'Finn Fitzgerald! My very own boss! *Boss* being the operative word!' She pouted. 'Because he always tells me what to do!'

He smiled back. 'Hello, Karolina. Is your mother here?'

Karolina pouted again. 'Why do you always ask me about my mother, for heaven's sake? We aren't joined at the hip, you know!'

'Because your mother is meant to be here chaperoning you,' he explained patiently.

'Oh, phooey to that! She's chatting up a man from one of the cable channels!' And Karolina grabbed a glass of champagne from a passing waiter.

Finn smoothly removed the glass from her hand and handed it to Amber. 'We'll take that,' he said. 'I can arrange for you to have a soft drink, if you like.'

'What—a bottle of milk?' snapped Karolina. 'Keep it!

I wonder, when are you going to learn that I'm not a child any more, Finn?' And she marched off as well as her spindly high heels would allow.

'When you stop behaving like one, I guess,' murmured Finn, as the three of them watched her sway her way to the other side of the room.

'Oh, dear,' commented Amber. 'Pep talk coming up, I fear.'

'Do they often come over like prima donnas?' asked Ursula, with interest.

Amber's attention was all on Finn, but his green eyes were busy following the progress of his newest and hottest model. 'Sometimes. Not often,' she answered, wondering why her heart remained so heavy. 'It's an occupational hazard, I'm afraid—though by no means the biggest one.'

Ursula, busy watching the proceedings with amusement, failed to notice the tortured note in her sister's voice. 'And what's the biggest one?'

'Oh, they fall in love with Finn,' answered Amber tonelessly. 'Only half the time he doesn't even see the danger. Or maybe he does,' she added suddenly, not caring what Ursula thought, not caring what anyone thought—not even Finn. Because right then her world seemed like a house of cards which was in danger of subsiding. 'Maybe he does,' she repeated quietly. 'And just pretends not to.'

But Finn wasn't even listening.

CHAPTER FIVE

AMBER woke up abruptly and lay very still, her body clock and the suffocating darkness telling her that it was extremely early in the morning, but that something else seemed very different too.

And then she remembered that it was Christmas morning. No wonder it felt so out of the ordinary!

Her mouth curved into a smile as she slowly turned her head to see whether Finn was still sleeping, and then the smile faded when she saw that his space in the bed was completely empty. Not just empty but unruffled, the sheets as smooth as a newly made hospital bed—as though he hadn't slept in it at all.

She glanced down at the clock which was gleaming red on the radio-alarm. Half-past four. She lay there for a moment and listened for the sound of him moving around, but, though she strained her ears, she could hear nothing. She let her eyes adjust to the darkness, then glanced around the room to see if there were any unaccustomed shapes lurking in any of the corners—shapes which resembled presents! But there was nothing. Which meant that he was probably wrapping last-minute gifts!

She stretched luxuriously beneath the cosy warmth of the duvet. So did she try to go straight back to sleep? Or go searching for Finn?

The deep jade folds of her clingy satin nightdress moulded themselves to her thighs as she stretched and climbed out of bed. Usually she started the night off wearing a nightdress, and then woke up in the morning completely naked—Finn having peeled the garment off some time during the night, before starting to make love to her.

But not last night.

It had been an odd Christmas Eve, with Finn holed up in his office until late. Like most of the world, Allure models and bookers and accountants did not work for the few days before and after Christmas, but two of their models had been involved in a serious accident. The light aircraft they'd been travelling in had crash-landed in the middle of the Australian desert ten days earlier. The pilot had been killed outright, and one of the models had broken her leg badly and lost a lot of blood.

Both women were now recovering well in hospital, but the crash had made a big story in the Australian press and Finn had flown over to offer his help and support. He'd even made the six o'clock news, with a breathy and beautiful blonde reporter firing questions at him, while Amber had watched the flickering TV screen in their flat, thousands of miles away.

He hadn't arrived home until the morning of Christmas Eve, jet-lagged and grumpy and distinctly thinner than when he had left, thanks to a bout of flu on his travels. Amber thought he should have gone straight to bed on his return, but he had insisted on wading through a pile of outstanding paperwork.

'Can't you leave that?' Amber had pleaded, but he had resolutely shaken his head.

'Not with Christmas coming up, I can't. The office is going to be shut for *days*, Amber—and it needs to be done.'

'Then let someone else do it, Finn. *Please*.'

'Amber,' he had sighed. 'There isn't anyone else to do it—Jackson's not back yet. And sometimes only the boss will do. *You* know that.'

Yeah, she knew that. As she knew that lately she

seemed to come very low down on Finn's list of priorities.

Deciding that his jet-lag must be responsible for such an uncharacteristically early rising, Amber yawned, pushed the sleep-tousled hair off her face and went in search of him.

She didn't have far to look. She found him sitting motionless in the darkness of the drawing room, hunched up in a chair and staring sightlessly into space. He had obviously just pulled on a pair of old jeans and a T-shirt, and his feet were bare.

Something in his posture made her heart contract with fear, and she stared at him in silence, strangely reluctant to disturb him.

But it seemed that he sensed her presence anyway, for he turned his head slightly to look at her, with fatigue stamped all over his hard profile. 'Hello, Amber,' he said slowly.

Was it her imagination, or did his voice sound *distant*—as if she were a woman he'd brought home for the night, without getting to know her properly?

'Everything okay?' she asked him hesitantly.

'Sure.' His gaze was steady. 'Why shouldn't it be?'

'Just that you're up very early.'

'I couldn't sleep.'

'You should have woken me.'

He raised his eyebrows. 'It seems I have.'

Jet-lag, Amber decided, her heart racing. It made people behave oddly. She forced herself to smile at him, determined to have a happy Christmas Day. 'Let me guess—you've just been wrapping my Christmas present?' she queried brightly.

He shook his head slowly as he gazed without emotion into her eyes. 'Actually, I haven't bought you one,' he told her slowly.

Amber tried to tell herself that it didn't matter. That Christmas had become an outrageous celebration of commercialisation which went completely against what lay at the heart of the festival itself. But somehow it *did* matter. Her bottom lip puckered. 'Oh,' she said.

'I'm sorry, sweetheart.' Finn rubbed at one of his temples with impatient fingers. 'Australia got in the way, and then I picked up that stupid bug and I didn't want to buy you any old thing, just for the sake of it—'

'Oh, please don't feel that you have to offer me excuses, Finn.' She gave a light little laugh which didn't sound like her laugh at all. 'You make me feel like a secretary whose boss has forgotten her at Christmas! I think I can just about cope with not getting a present from you.' But she wondered why he hadn't got up, or taken her into his arms, or...

The piercing shriek of the telephone startled them both.

Finn scowled. 'What the hell—?'

'Bad news,' gulped Amber instantly as she quickly went to pick it up.

'Leave it, will you, Amber? I'll take it!' Finn's voice was brusque and authoritative as he began to lever himself stiffly out of the chair, like a novice runner the day after a marathon.

Amber took one look at him and glared. 'Oh, for goodness' sake!' she snapped. 'You're still half dead on your feet from jet-lag! I think I can cope with the phone, even if it *is* bad news!' But she didn't say what was uppermost in her mind as she picked the receiver up— that Finn was the one with elderly parents and a huge extended family living in Ireland. And that if it *was* bad news, it was more likely to concern him.

'Hello,' she said, and then had her ear half deafened by the sound of hysterical female sobs. 'Hello?' she repeated. 'Who is this, please?' But the unintelligible crying continued. Finn was by her side now and she gave him a bewildered shrug.

He took the receiver from her but, even so, the sobbing was still audible to Amber.

'Finn Fitzgerald here,' he said. 'Who's speaking?'

Amber heard the crying lessen in volume in response to the honeyed balm of his voice, and he listened intently, then nodded.

'So what have you done?' he asked. 'Good. No! Stay there. Don't worry. *No!*' Now his voice sounded harsh. 'Don't do that! I'll be right over.' He put the phone down and stared at Amber, her face snow-white, her sapphire eyes like ebony-centred saucers.

'What's happened? Who was it?'

'Birgitta,' he told her reluctantly.

'*Birgitta?*' she echoed in disbelief. 'What the hell is Birgitta doing calling us *here* at this time in the morning? On Christmas *Day!*'

'Well, it sure as hell wasn't to chat about the weather!' he snapped. 'Or to wish us a happy holiday!'

Amber's heart raced with anger and humiliation—as much at the scowling look on his face as at the put-down. 'I wasn't for a minute suggesting that it was,' she told him icily. 'Is there some kind of problem with the flat?'

'Obviously,' he returned shortly. 'There's water coming through the ceiling from the bathroom—and there's no way she can get a plumber now.'

'So naturally she turned to *you*, did she? Dear, darling Finn—who seems capable of getting most things in a crisis!' she snapped, unable to keep the sarcasm from her voice.

'Of course she turned to me!' he exploded. 'What else

did you expect her to do? Allure *does* happen to own the flat! And neither of them know anyone in London—'

'So why didn't they go back to Sweden?' she sniped nastily. 'It *is* Christmas, after all!'

The look he gave her was withering. 'I can't believe you just said that, Amber,' he told her quietly. 'The reason they're in London is because Karolina has to fly out to Barbados tomorrow—'

'Such a tough life!' Amber gave an exaggerated sigh.

'I think it *is* tough when fame comes so young and so easy,' he told her slowly. 'It can detonate the whole infrastructure of your life.' He met her angry look with a level stare. 'Look—I told her that I'd go over.'

'I know you did. I was standing right here listening, remember? Birgitta is a grown woman, isn't she? Why can't she cope?'

Finn's mouth twisted. 'Call me old-fashioned, if you like, but I happen to be one of those people who think that men handle certain crises better than women—and leaking ceilings is one of them!'

'Then why isn't *Mr* Lindberg around to sort all this out?' she raged. 'It's Christmas *morning* for goodness' sake! Doesn't Birgitta's husband miss her? Doesn't Karolina miss her father?'

'I told you—Birgitta and her husband have separated,' he clipped out. 'Temporarily.'

'Oh, it's always "temporarily"!' put in Amber caustically. 'The word suggests that the marriage will automatically get better—whereas in reality it's usually a convenient excuse for a woman out looking to find a replacement man!'

'They're actually having a pretty miserable time of it, all told,' he told her coldly.

The icy disapproval on his face made Amber's heart

lurch in alarm, and fear made her even more mean-spirited. 'Oh, I'm so *sorry* to hear that!'

'The sentiment would be nice if I thought for a moment that you meant it, Amber.'

'Well, you'd better go charging round to their rescue, hadn't you?' She smiled insincerely. 'I hope you fed your white horse his oats last night! Oh, and Ursula's arriving for Christmas lunch at twelve—in case you'd forgotten. So try not to be *too* late!' And she headed off towards the kitchen without a backward glance.

She clattered around with cups and saucers, ostensibly making herself a pot of tea, but in reality she was listening out for Finn, and when the front door slammed shut without him having come in to say sorry—or even goodbye—she felt like bursting into tears. She briefly thought about going back to bed, but knew for certain that she would be unable to sleep.

Instead, she took her tea into the drawing room and drew the curtains back to watch the sun come up. The windows were as large as a cinema screen, and she sat in front of them feeling very small and isolated.

It was a strange time and a strange day to be on her own. There were none of the usual sounds of dawn breaking over London. No milk floats out, with their bottles clanking noisily in crates. No distant rumble of lorries and cars, as early drivers began to populate the roads in an attempt to beat the traffic. Instead, there was complete and utter silence outside.

And it wasn't as though she could ring anyone. Just who *could* you ring at five-thirty on Christmas morning? Her sister, sure, if it was a real emergency. But it was not a real emergency—it was more a case of appalling jealousy, and Ursula would probably tell her to pull herself together and not to be so stupid.

Because what was she actually jealous *of*?

Surely she didn't think that Finn would allow himself to be ensnared by a sixteen-year-old model who had a crush on him, however beautiful she was? Or her mother—just as beautiful—and much closer in age to Finn.

Amber put her mug of tea down, her hand shaking violently. Women came on strong to Finn. That was a fact—a fact he had acknowledged at the time of their engagement. He was always going to appear sexy and desirable to the opposite sex—but that didn't mean that he was about to start taking up any of the offers which came his way. Either she trusted him or she didn't—and if she didn't trust him then she should extricate herself from the relationship. Fast.

Because otherwise she could drive herself quite mad with her fears and suspicions.

The seconds and the minutes ticked by interminably, and Amber was reduced to switching on television and tuning into one of the many breakfast shows—something she never normally had the time nor the inclination to do. But the presenters were being relentlessly cheerful—their brittle-bright smiles and inane chatter making Amber's already stretched nerves jangle even more—and after five minutes she switched the set off.

She sat staring at her own Christmas tree, and the shiny presents stacked beneath it. Gifts for both of them, sent over from Ireland by his family. And there were little things, too—bought for them by the staff at Allure. And, inevitably, there were gifts for Finn alone, from some of the models.

But none for her, from Finn.

She thought about the new skis she had bought for him, which Ursula would be bringing over with her at lunchtime. She had wrapped them and taken them to Ursula's flat because their shape had been too much of a give-away for Amber to risk trying to hide them around their flat! She had bought him cashmere socks too, and chocolate-covered macadamia nuts—his favourite—and some sexy silk boxer shorts in an outrageous crimson colour. She had imagined him trying them on...and her taking them off again...

Amber swallowed down the first hint of tears and switched the radio on instead. A Christmas service was being broadcast and the sound of the carols made her feel unbearably nostalgic, but at least they focussed her mind. She showered and dressed and forced herself to put on the gold tunic dress and apply some make-up to her face.

When she was wrapped up in a warm, mock fur-trimmed velvet coat, she left the flat and stepped outside into the bitter chill, where a meagre amount of snow-flakes were fluttering down, as though the sky couldn't bear to let them go. She turned her collar up, and set off for church.

The service was wonderful, but poignant, and Amber found herself missing her mother more than ever.

She sang her heart out during the carols, and when the congregation filed out almost an hour later the snow had begun to settle. The soft white mantle gave the city a curiously clean and pure look, and Amber felt her heart lift unexpectedly as she shook the hand of the priest who had taken the service.

He sent a rueful glance up at the heavy grey sky. 'Looks like the bookies will be set to lose a fortune!' he commented irreverently.

Amber knotted her scarf firmly around her neck, only half listening. 'And why's that, Father?'

The priest shook his head in mock dismay. 'Do you young folk never read the betting news? The odds were stacked firmly against a white Christmas—heaven knows, I've lost a good few pounds myself!' he informed her, with a twinkling smile which made Amber wonder whether or not he was joking!

She slithered her way back to the flat to find that Finn still wasn't home—but at least church had put things in some kind of perspective. Would she really have wanted to be tied to a man who would suggest that a sixteen-year-old and her mother go and find their *own* plumber? On Christmas morning? Finn was doing no more than she would have expected him to do under the circumstances—she really shouldn't chastise him for playing the good Samaritan. And when he came back she would tell him so...

She turned the central heating up and touched up her make-up, and then, after she had manoeuvred the huge turkey into the oven, she started peeling the vegetables.

She had just cut a cross into the last Brussels sprout when the doorbell rang, and, thinking it must be Ursula, struggling under the weight of the skis, Amber rushed to answer it. Her sister was early.

But it wasn't Ursula.

Standing on the step, the upper part of his body almost completely obscured by foliage, stood Finn, weighed down by the countless blooms he was holding in his arms.

There were hothouse flowers of every variety and every hue—more flowers than Amber could ever remember seeing. Peach-coloured roses and pure white lilies. Deep-blue cornflowers and fragrant ice-pink frangipani. There were palest freesia and waxy stephanotis. Scarlet peonies and early narcissi. The sight and the smell of the massed blossoms assailed Amber's senses and her mouth fell open in wonder as she stared at him.

Green eyes sparked loving fire at her over the rainbow

petals and Amber just stood there, afraid to speak for a moment, in case she should start crying.

'Finn?' was all she could manage.

He walked straight past her like a man on a mission and deposited all the flowers in a great heap on the dining-room table, and then he came back to where she still stood, framed in the doorway.

'W-what are all these flowers for?' she wanted to know, but he shook his head.

Gently closing the door, he wordlessly took her into his arms and held her tightly as he buried his face in the fragrance of her hair. It seemed a long time before he spoke. 'You know what they're for, Amber,' he told her, his voice muffled against the top of her head. 'They're nothing but an inadequate token of my love for you, sweetheart.'

Amber's eyes closed in relief, her arms tightening fiercely across the broad expanse of his back, her fingers slithering over the leather flying jacket which he wore, and she didn't want to speak again. Didn't want to break this spell, this sense of having reached some kind of watershed where nameless fears would not touch her again.

Eventually he raised his head and lifted her chin with a gentle finger, capturing her eyes with his glittering gaze, and Amber was shaken by the conflict she saw written in the grass-green depths.

'What?' she whispered, as softly as if she had been back in church. 'What is it, darling Finn?'

He shook his head, as though her simple question had wounded him, and she would have unsaid her words if she could.

'Tell me,' she urged. 'If there's some kind of problem, then just come out and *tell* me. That's what I'm here for.'

He hesitated. 'I've been unbearable to live with,' he said suddenly. 'Foul and grumpy and bad-tempered.'

Amber felt as though a heavy weight had been lifted from her shoulders. Was *that* all? But she also remembered the desolation she had felt building up over the past few weeks. She didn't want to string him up for his behaviour, but she sure as hell wasn't going to condone it! This was the first really bad row of their relationship, and how she handled it would affect how they handled their disagreements in the future.

She glanced up at him from between the protective shield of her eyelashes, searching for the right blend of understanding and forgiveness. 'Do you want me to disagree with you, Finn Fitzgerald?'

He laughed, but the self-recrimination which coloured the sound of his laughter was unmistakable. 'No. I don't want you to do that, Amber O'Neil,' he murmured back, with some of his habitual mocking humour.

'Well, do you want to tell me why you've been acting the way you have?'

'Overwork, I guess. I think we both need a holiday.'

Amber looked at him in delight. 'Seriously?'

'Seriously.' He sighed. 'I just never dreamed that the agency would grow as big as it has done.'

'It's going to grow even bigger if Jackson gets his own way about opening up a branch in New York.'

'Yeah,' he commented thoughtfully, and tried to stifle a yawn.

She put her hand up to his mouth and he kissed each fingertip in turn.

'Maybe you should skip having a New Year party this year?'

He shook his dark head. 'Then it wouldn't be a proper Christmas, would it?' he teased as he pulled her even closer.

'Things have been crazy at Allure for too long now,' he whispered against her ear. 'I guess you shouldn't knock success when it comes, but you spend a long time waiting for it to arrive, and when it does you realise that there's a price to pay. And something has to give—'

'But hopefully not you,' she murmured into the warm haven of his neck.

He didn't answer for a moment. 'Hopefully not me,' he agreed.

'I went to church while you were out,' she told him suddenly.

He raised his eyebrows. 'And did you pray for forgiveness?'

'I prayed for *your* forgiveness!'

He laughed at this. 'Wise move.'

Amber forced herself to ask the question which would demonstrate that she was a nice, rounded, thoughtful human being, instead of a mean-spirited and possessive one. 'And did you...did you sort out the leaking ceiling okay?'

He hesitated.

'At the flat,' she elaborated. 'For Karolina and her mum?'

There was a slight pause. 'Yeah. An emergency plumber was arriving as I left.'

'So soon?' Amber was impressed. 'How did you manage that?'

'By promising to pay an exorbitant amount of money for his call-out fee,' he told her drily. 'Though, to be fair, who wants to be called out early on Christmas morning?'

Resisting the impulse to say that *he* hadn't minded, Amber delved deeper into her dwindling supply of kind-heartedness. 'And w-what about lunch?'

He looked surprised. 'I thought you had all that sorted out?'

'I have. I have. It's just, I wondered what Karolina and her mother were doing. It won't be much fun if they're pulling crackers while water drips onto their heads!'

He shook his head. 'Oh, no—that's okay. I already invited them, but they're apparently going to eat a magnificent meal at the Granchester.'

'Oh, what a shame,' said Amber, with as much feeling as she could manage.

He glanced over to the table, where the discarded blooms lay in a fragrant and psychedelic heap. 'And, in the meantime, hadn't we better do something with these flowers? Unless we want tulips sharing a plate with our turkey! Do you have a vase?'

Amber forced herself to snap into festive mode. 'I have several. But somehow I don't think that several are going to be enough! Never mind—we can always use milk bottles! And I'd better start—this is going to be a long operation!'

'I'll help you,' he said slowly, and she was aware that his eyes were following her almost obsessively as she moved across the room.

They worked companionably, putting the flowers into any vessel which could conceivably pass as a vase until almost every surface in the flat contained a spray of blooms. It was a heady smell and an enchanting sight. Amber leaned back against Finn as they surveyed their handiwork, then gave a sigh of satisfaction.

'Looks like a movie star's boudoir,' she observed.

'Too much?'

'Totally,' she agreed gravely. 'But if you can't be extravagant on Christmas Day, then when can you? Speaking of which—' She glanced down at her watch and gave a squeak of horror. 'Oh, my goodness—look at the time! Ursula will be here soon and I haven't even made the stuffing!'

But he shook his head and took her by the hand. 'Not yet,' he said.

'But, Finn—'

'It'll wait,' he told her firmly as he led her over to one of the giant sofas.

But Amber shook her head. 'No, Finn, sweetheart,' she objected reluctantly. 'There isn't time. Ursula will be here soon and I don't want to be scrabbling around for my clothes when she does. Not on Christmas Day.'

His smile was sadness and tenderness mixed. 'You think that whenever I touch you I only want to make love?'

She gave him a long look. '*We-ll,*' she drawled, her mouth curving into an unstoppable smile. 'Usually. Yes—I suppose I do. I think I'd probably worry if you didn't.'

'Well, you don't have to worry, sweetheart,' he murmured meltingly, as he sat down on the sofa and drew her onto his lap. 'I'm not going to make love to you now.'

'You're not?'

'Of course I'm not! You just told me that there wasn't time—you contrary creature!'

'You could at least *try!*'

'You enjoy slapping me down, do you?'

'Mmm. Damned right I do! I enjoy delayed gratification, too!' She bared her small teeth into a mock snarl, then kissed the tip of his nose as she looked at him thoughtfully. 'Well, if you haven't brought me over here to make love to me, Finn—then just what *have* you got in mind?'

There was a pause. 'I just want to hold you,' he said,

in a voice which sounded laden with regret, and a brief foreboding flickered its dark shadow over Amber. She clung onto him like a limpet without knowing why.

When Ursula rang the doorbell, bang on the stroke of midday, they were still sitting on the sofa together, wrapped in each other's arms like teenage sweethearts.

Amber wouldn't let Finn get up—she didn't want him seeing her present until she was ready. 'You've got to stay right there and keep your eyes closed!' she told him. 'While Ursula and I bring your present in!'

She opened the door to her sister, her eyes lighting up when she saw that Ursula had somehow managed to manoeuvre the carefully wrapped skis up the stairs.

Amber put her finger over her lips. 'How did you manage to get those up here without help?' she whispered, trying very hard not to laugh.

'A very helpful taxi driver,' said Ursula, 'who was obviously susceptible to generous female curves!'

Amber ran her eyes over her sister, who was wearing a seasonal red jersey dress beneath her camel coat. The dress *did* make her look curvy, but the colour accentuated the dark sheen of her raven hair and the clear, berry-stained beauty of her skin. Her deep blue eyes sparkled with health and life, and, not for the first time, Amber found herself silently cursing Ursula's boss.

If only Ursula would stop comparing all men to Ross Sheridan, Amber thought crossly—then she might be able to settle down with someone else and find contentment.

'I'm not surprised he was so helpful,' commented Amber truthfully. 'You look absolutely stunning!'

'Do I? *Honestly?*'

Amber knew a moment of sheer fury. Had no man ever complimented her sister? What was the *matter* with a society which only saw beauty as a universal shape which was contrary to a woman's *natural* shape? 'Cross my heart and hope to die.' She smiled. 'Come on, let's drag the skis in first—I left Finn sitting on the sofa with his eyes closed. If we stand here nattering for much longer he'll have fallen asleep!'

Carefully, they steered the garishly wrapped skis in through the front door, guided them round the old-fashioned hatstand, which Amber had bought and which Finn detested, until they brought them to a rest in front of the sofa.

Finn lay on his back now, sprawled out with careless abandon, wearing the black jeans which were his trade mark—today teamed with a black sweater in the lightest, softest cashmere, which clung lovingly to every muscle and sinew of his hard torso. His dark head rested on a cushion of kingfisher-blue, and his face looked remarkably pale against the bright, intense colour. The ebony arc of his lashes only emphasised his pallor, and once again Amber vowed that—whatever Finn said about business projections—she was *not* going to let him work so hard, come the New Year.

'You can open your eyes now, Finn,' she called to him softly, but he didn't respond.

Ursula frowned as she watched the steady rise and fall of his chest. 'He's fallen asleep,' she observed in surprise.

Amber shook her head. 'No. He's just pretending. He was awake just a minute ago.' She winked hugely at her sister. 'Do you think this bra is just too risqué, Ursula? Shows too much of my breasts, do you think?' But still Finn did not respond.

Ursula leaned over him. 'I tell you, Amber—he's asleep. He's not faking it.' Her blue eyes twinkled in a determined attempt to hide her embarrassment. She might be the least worldly-wise woman on the planet, but even *she* knew what caused men to fall asleep so suddenly in the middle of the day. 'What *have* you been doing to him?'

'Nothing. I swear. He was awake just a minute ago.' Confused, and feeling out of her depth, Amber bent over to give his shoulder a gentle shake. It took a couple of seconds before the sinfully long lashes fluttered open and his eyes focussed on her, first in befuddlement and then in a state of mystification.

He sat up quickly. 'What's going on?'

Amber clapped the back of her hand dramatically to her forehead and pretended to swoon. 'Masked raiders entered the flat!' she declared dramatically. 'They coshed you over the head and then—'

'What *happened*, Amber?' he interrogated urgently.

Amber blinked. 'You fell asleep,' she told him lamely. 'That's all.'

'That's all?' He rubbed at his brow distractedly and gave a tiny shake of his head, as if trying to clear it. 'What the hell am I doing, falling asleep in the middle of the day?'

Ursula was watching them both very closely. 'Do you feel okay, Finn?'

'Of course I feel okay!'

Amber squeezed his arm. 'There's no need to be so defensive, darling,' she told him soothingly. 'You're obviously still jet-lagged.'

His green eyes gleamed with a certain kind of relief. 'Yeah,' he drawled, and allowed himself a lazy yawn. 'I always tend to underestimate the effect of crossing time zones.'

'And you had that flu bug out in Australia,' Amber put in. '*And* you were stressed out before you left!'

Finn winked at Ursula. 'See how decrepit your sister makes me out to be! Happy Christmas, Ursula!'

Ursula gave a laugh. 'Happy Christmas!' Her eyes sparkled. 'I don't think Amber thinks of you as particularly decrepit, Finn.' She stared meaningfully at her sister, then at the cumbersome present still lying at their feet. 'Not when you see what she's bought you for Christmas!'

Amber thought about picking the skis up, then thought better of it. 'Happy Christmas, darling,' she murmured as he looked down and noticed them at last.

'What *can* these be?' he mused, his grin all crooked.

Sensing that Finn would want to start kissing Amber without an audience, Ursula beat a hasty retreat for the door. 'I'll bring the other presents in,' she called, sniffing the air like a puppy as she went. 'What a lot of flowers you've got, Amber! Who did they all come from?'

Amber and Finn met each other's eyes. 'It's a long story!' they said, in unison.

CHAPTER SIX

AMBER bit into her croissant and black cherry jam squished out of the sides. She wiped her finger all along the jammy bulge and then licked it luxuriously, to find Finn leaning back against the pillows watching her, the newspapers lying in front of him unread.

Thinking that the brooding look in his green eyes might be hunger of the more conventional nature, she offered him the croissant. 'Like a bite?'

He shook his head and a small muscle began to work in his cheek. 'No, thanks,' he drawled, and his eyes flickered over the plate she had balanced rather precariously on her knees. He frowned. 'And I don't particularly want jam and crumbs spread all over the sheets either, if you don't mind, Amber.'

Amber blinked at him in surprise. There was no need to say it like that! As though she were some incompetent little minion who was messing up his space! 'Sor*ry*!' She thought how stony his voice sounded this morning! In fact, he'd been like a bear with a sore head ever since he had opened his eyes.

Determined to wipe that rather sour look from his face, she fixed him with her most beguiling look. 'Maybe I should have asked your permission to eat breakfast in bed,' she joked purringly over her shoulder.

He didn't respond.

She tried provocatively licking a sticky splotch of black cherry from the side of her mouth, her eyes fixed firmly on him as she slowly ran her tongue around her lips. It wasn't the most original come-on in the world,

101

but it was usually effective. And she badly wanted Finn to make love to her. He hadn't touched her since Christmas Day. True, that was only three days ago—but that was a lifetime compared to the frequency with which they usually had sex.

'Finn?' she murmured softly, and she rested her elbow on her pillow as she turned to face him.

'And now you're scattering crumbs everywhere!' he observed with a scowl.

'That's not what you *used* to say,' she objected, hurt, and not caring if she showed it. 'When we started living together!'

His broad, naked shoulders were shrugged in a dismissive gesture. 'We used to lie around in bed for days and have non-stop sex when we started our affair.' He yawned. 'But surely you're not suggesting that we should spend the rest of our lives doing that?'

She met the cool question in his eyes and was momentarily bewildered by it before answering him as honestly as she could. 'Why not?' she quizzed softly. '*I've* certainly no objections to doing that. Everything I've ever read about maintaining a successful sex-life says that you have to keep the interest alive. And if we like lying around in bed having sex all the time, then why change it?'

'Oh, for goodness' sake, Amber—don't be so naive!' He ran an impatient hand back through his already ruffled dark hair. 'Things can't *possibly* stay the same! Relationships change—'

'Just w-what are you saying, exactly?' Amber demanded, suddenly feeling panicked—not so much by his words but by that unfamiliar look which had made his eyes appear positively glacial.

He folded up his unread newspaper and placed it on

the floor beside the bed. 'I'm saying that when a couple start having an affair—'

'I do wish you wouldn't keep using that word,' she interrupted crossly. 'It makes what we're doing sound illicit—and it isn't! "Affair" is a word I associate with seedy little extra-marital relationships, and we happen to be engaged to be married!' She waved her diamond ring under his nose to add weight to her argument.

'Oh, for heaven's sake, Amber!' he exploded. 'Just stick to the point, can't you? I did not intend for a simple request to reduce your crumb-scattering to develop into a discussion on semantics!'

'Then just what *did* you intend it to develop into?' she shot back icily. 'A friendly conversation? A serene and trouble-free morning?'

He sighed. 'I was simply trying to explain that some of those little foibles of yours which I found so enchanting at the start of this *relationship*,' he emphasised, with heavy sarcasm, 'might have the ability to irritate me in the future, that's all.'

'That's *all*?' she repeated in disbelief.

'Well, is it really such a terrible crime for me to suggest that you don't spread crumbs and jam everywhere? Particularly in bed.'

Amber's eyes widened. 'I can't believe I'm hearing correctly! This—*this*—coming from the man who used to ask me to spray whipped cream over certain parts of his anatomy and then spend as long as possible licking it off? You certainly weren't bothered about the state of the sheets *then*!'

'That's *different*!' he snapped back.

'*How* is it different?'

'When I started having sex with you—' He must have seen the shocked look on her face, because he immediately amended his words. 'Okay, honey—maybe I'd better rephrase that to your satisfaction. When I started having a *relationship* with you—'

Amber's skin crawled at the cavalier and sarcastic way he had chosen to describe her sexual awakening, and maybe that was what prompted her to say sulkily, 'You mean—when you took my virginity?'

Finn nodded slowly, his green eyes never leaving her face. 'Yeah. I guess that's one way of putting it—if you want to turn this into a power struggle,' he drawled softly. 'Although, as I recall, I didn't do so much taking as you did *giving*—isn't that right, Amber?'

She supposed that if he had said it in a loving way then it might almost have been considered a compliment. But he didn't say it in a loving way. In fact, he said it with all the repressed and negative emotion of a bank clerk informing a customer of an outstanding overdraft they had no hope of settling.

'Well, it's true that I must have made it transparently clear that I wanted you, but what did you want from our first encounter?' she demanded. 'A battle royal before my unwilling surrender?'

'Hardly.'

'Well, what, then?'

He shook his head wearily. 'It doesn't matter.'

'It does matter!' She sat bolt-upright in bed and the plate went flying among the folds of the snow-white duvet.

'Now look what you've done,' he observed caustically.

But Amber could make out a certain sense of triumph in his words. Once upon a time he wouldn't have even *looked* at the scattered bits of jammy croissant—he would have been too busy ogling the satin and lace of her creamy nightgown as it strained against the lush pull of her breasts. 'Okay, you've won!' she spat at him. 'I'll never eat food in bed again! Okay?'

She fell back down again, burying her face in her pillow, disastrously close to tears, but she was confused more than anything else. Why was he *acting* this way? Chipping away at her composure? She held her breath, expecting him to start caressing her shoulders in the way he had done so often before if they had exchanged angry words.

Yet these words seemed to have cut deeper than any previous ones had ever done. Even worse than the things they had said to one another on Christmas morning. She was left feeling as though she were stranded on a ledge, high up on a mountain, with Finn separated and miles away from her.

She rolled onto her back and grabbed a tissue from the box on the locker, blew her nose and looked up at him.

'Remember Christmas Day?' she asked him.

She saw an unfamiliar impatience on his face. 'It was three days ago—I haven't been afflicted with short-term memory loss just *yet*.' He frowned. 'What about it?'

She tried to keep calm. Nothing was going to be gained by her being crotchety with him. 'Do you remember saying how grumpy you'd been? How difficult you'd been to live with?'

His gaze was cool. 'Did I?'

Her good intentions flew straight out of the window, and she waved her hands impatiently in the air. 'Damn it, Finn—you *know* you did! Are you being deliberately obtuse?'

The movements she had made caused her breasts to jiggle beneath their thin confinement, and she heard him suck in a deep, ragged breath. Amber saw that his darkened eyes were mesmerised by the thrust of her nipples against the lace, and she wondered if he was going to just pull her into his arms and peel the nightgown from her body, to start making slow, irresistible love to her.

But he didn't.

Amber glanced down at her fingers, which were anxiously knotted together on the snowy backdrop of the duvet, and the diamond which glittered on her third finger mocked her in all its stony-hard beauty. Why on earth had he bothered buying the wretched ring and proposing in the first place? When had Finn last mentioned marriage? she found herself wondering—then despaired of herself for being so submissive. When had *she*?

Finn had been flying to Australia, collapsing with the flu and getting up at the crack of dawn to fix Birgitta and Karolina's leaking ceiling. So what had happened to all her confidence? To all the breezy light-heartedness which had attracted this gorgeous man to her in the first place? She had whittled away at it with all her nagging self-doubts and insecurities, hadn't she? And no one could deny that Finn had contributed to *those*.

'Finn—'

He turned around, the golden cream of his skin as smooth and delicious as the most expensive fudge. 'What?'

She screwed up her face in frustration at his indifference. 'Something's wrong—I know it is.'

Wariness flickered across his eyes. 'Such as?'

'Well, I know you're working too hard—'

He elevated his eyebrows unhelpfully. 'But not right now, sugar.'

'No.' She tried again, plucking up the courage to say what had been buzzing her mind with doubts for weeks now. 'We haven't really discussed the wedding lately, either.'

He gave a half-laugh. 'Well, *you* have, remember?

That illuminating interview you gave to *Wow!* magazine?'

Amber swallowed down a sigh of impatience. 'You're not *still* holding that against me, are you?'

'I'm trying not to,' he told her truthfully. 'But to be perfectly honest just the thought of it makes me cringe. It's ironic, really—I've spent the whole of my life forging a persona for myself which has been publicity-free, which is not easy in this business. Not easy at all.' He paused. 'And then you come along and blow it all in one afternoon.'

'Are you still trying to make me feel bad?'

'I'm trying to tell you how *I* feel. I can't help it if you don't like what you hear. You were the one who asked me, Amber.'

So did that mean she *shouldn't* have asked? Simply pretend that nothing was wrong? But surely that would be no good either. Something was gnawing away at the heart of their relationship, and if she didn't get to the bottom of it soon...

She had been *intending* to ask him whether a spring wedding was out of the question, but one glance at the frosty distance in his eyes changed her mind.

She played Little Miss Housewife instead.

'Like some more coffee?' she asked brightly.

'Sounds like a good idea.' He picked up the discarded plate and began deliberately piling it with all the buttery fragments of pastry. 'Don't bother bringing it back in here—I'll come and drink it in the kitchen.' He handed her the plate. 'Do you want to take your rubbish with you?'

'Right.' White-faced and trembling, she marched out of the bedroom, not wanting him to see the depth of her distress. Today was a holiday, so they could have lain in all day if they'd wanted. No need to go anywhere—

particularly in view of his expressed need to rest. So why was he getting up with that sour expression on his face, as if he had the world to run and all the cares to go with it?

As Amber ground the coffee beans, she felt her composure slipping away.

Finn took absolutely ages, but at least by the time he wandered out in his oldest pair of black jeans and a black T-shirt—which gave him a devilish look—Amber had recovered something of her self-possession.

She had her eyes closed as she sniffed at the fragrant coffee, and when she opened them it was to find Finn standing watching her. Some of the coldness had gone from his eyes, and his mouth was kiss-tender, so that hers found itself instinctively responding with a soft, curving smile. What she wanted was to run up to him and hurl herself into his arms, and ask him to tell her that nothing was wrong and that everything was going to be all right. But she didn't dare.

She didn't dare because she was frightened of what the answer might be.

Instead, she poured them both a coffee, then perched on one of the bar stools. She stared at the winter-flowering jasmine which stood in a pot on the side, deliberately not glancing in Finn's direction—rather as people did when they wanted to engage a child or an animal. Ignoring them and discounting their unease, knowing it would draw them to you.

And it did.

He came over and levered himself up to perch on one of the tall stools opposite hers, tucking his long legs up onto one of the rungs. But he was silent as he picked up his coffee and cupped it between his palms, staring intently at the circling brown liquid as though he were searching for gold in the bottom of the cup. Fear gripped her again, but she forced herself to look at the facts, and the facts certainly weren't fearful. For some reason Finn was distracted, and she wasn't exactly helping matters by circling him like a cat preying on a bird.

If something was wrong then she'd find out what it was soon enough, and in the meantime she would forget weddings and just give him some space. They'd talk about normal stuff instead. Christmas stuff.

Amber took a sip of coffee and stared at him over the rim of her cup. 'Have you rung round about New Year's Eve yet?'

The pause while she waited for him to answer was so long that for a moment Amber wondered whether he had actually heard her.

'No,' he said eventually.

'Better get a move on, then! You know people keep their diaries free, hoping for an invite.'

'Yeah.' But his sigh sounded reluctant, and she knew that she hadn't imagined it.

New Year's Eve at Finn Fitzgerald's was something of a tradition—the only party he threw all year, and even people who should have known better found themselves clamouring for an invitation. He invited people who amused or interested him, and—since the numbers always varied—no two years were ever the same.

Except in one respect—that the entertainment never differed, with Finn always playing a couple of pieces on the piano. It had started out as an impromptu session years ago, before Amber had ever gone to work at Allure, and had proved so popular that his guests had insisted on an annual performance.

Although Finn had talent, he was not a natural performer—that was one of the reasons he had given up modelling. He always played the same two pieces, which he claimed were the only two he *could* play, and he always finished just in time for the bells chiming in the New Year. Usually he spent the last couple of weeks of December practising the pieces whenever he got the opportunity, but Amber now realised that she hadn't heard him playing.

Not once.

Apprehension gripped her.

'You *are* still planning to have a party?'

'Sure. I told you that the other day.'

Her lips were paper-dry. 'Just that I haven't heard you practising—'

He smiled, but it was a slick, professional smile—the type he sometimes switched on when he was working. 'That doesn't necessarily mean that I *haven't* been playing, does it? Just that you haven't been around to hear it.'

'Please don't patronise me, Finn!'

'Was I?' His expression remained bland. 'I wasn't aware that I *was* patronising you.'

She put her cup down with a shaking hand. 'Are we having *another* argument?' she demanded. 'Two in one morning—that must be a record!'

He shrugged as though he didn't particularly care. 'But adults don't always agree on every subject, do they? Even ones who live together.'

But we do! she wanted to shout at him. *We* agree on almost every subject—or at least I *thought* we did!

But something in his eyes stopped her, and Amber had the strong sense of needing to draw back, suspecting that if she pushed him into a corner, he might...just might...

But she was unable to even acknowledge what was bothering her, and, loathing herself for her compliance, she smiled at him instead. 'So *have* you been practising?' she questioned brightly, her smile so brittle she felt as though her lips might crack. 'Secretly?' What an actress she had become! She sounded as though she would be *overjoyed* if he told her that, yes—he had!

Was it her imagination, or did Finn look almost *disappointed*? Disappointed that she hadn't risen to the provocation? she wondered.

'No, I haven't been practising,' he growled out repressively. 'Oddly enough, I haven't really had the chance, in between flying to Australian hospitals and sorting out plumbing jobs!'

'Well, hadn't you better practise today?' she suggested mildly. 'You know how you like to polish those two particular pieces so that you sound like a world-class virtuoso! It's your need for perfection, Finn—that's what drives you!'

He slammed down his coffee cup and the sound was almost deafening. '*I'll* decide when *I* practise!' he snarled. 'And it ain't going to be today—'

He got up swiftly, his body stiffening as if for fight, and Amber stared up at him, her eyes darkening in alarm. 'W-why not today?' she stammered, too concerned to question the outrageously rude way in which he had spoken to her.

'Because I'm going into the office today!'

'But, Finn,' she objected, 'you've been complaining how hard you've been working!'

'No, honey,' he corrected grimly. '*You're* the one who has been complaining, not me.'

Her mouth fell open in the way she had thought mouths only did in cartoons as he strode out of the kitchen without another word.

CHAPTER SEVEN

'URSULA, *please*—you've *got* to come!'

Ursula's sigh was heavy down the telephone. 'Amber, I can't. I told you. I'm going on a winter holiday.'

Amber stared at her frightened, pale face reflected back at her from the mirror which hung in the hall. 'But you *never* go on winter holidays!'

'I know.' Ursula's voice was grim. 'I never go skiing, either. I never go on dates. I never pluck my eyebrows or eat breakfast in bed—'

'Well, I don't advise trying *that*,' put in Amber darkly.

'And I'll be thirty before long—'

'Not for another two years,' Amber pointed out in some alarm. 'And you mustn't start thinking like that! You're only as young as you feel!' When Ursula talked about getting old, it made *her* feel old. And getting older held even less appeal than usual when the whole substance of your future seemed to be shifting like quicksand...

'Whatever,' said Ursula, slightly dismissively. 'It's time I started doing all the things I've always wanted to do, instead of constantly putting my life on hold.'

'And is there a reason for this sudden change of heart?'

There was a pause. 'There is, but I'd rather not talk about it.'

'Is this something to do with Ross Sheridan?'

'No comment,' offered Ursula drily. 'Listen, Amber, I really have to run.'

'Of course,' said Amber, trying not to sound irritated,

though she knew she had no earthly right to be. She just wasn't used to *Ursula* being in a hurry with *her*, that was all. *She* was the one who was normally dashing to this and that and the other. Ursula was her big sister, who always had unlimited time and patience for her. But not any more, it seemed. 'I wish you *were* coming,' she said, in a little-girl voice.

'But why?' laughed Ursula. 'You don't need *me* to hold your hand! It's Finn's New Year party and you're his *fiancée* now. Just think of all the jealous looks you'll get! All those women casting daggers at you and wondering what you've got which has managed to ensnare one of London's most eligible bachelors!'

'I sometimes find myself wondering that,' said Amber gloomily.

'If that's an attempt to get me to sing your many praises, then I'm afraid I haven't time,' said Ursula.

'No.'

Ursula's voice changed when she heard the hollow little response. 'Amber, it's not like you to agree with me—nothing's *wrong*, is it?'

Once upon a time Amber might have said, yes, everything was wrong. But she was a grown woman now, one who had to handle her own life and its inevitable problems. She couldn't go running to her big sister every time things weren't going quite to her liking. And anyway—what could she possibly say to the sister she suspected deep down might still be a virgin?

That Finn hadn't come near her for days? That his moods had been black and unrecognisable? That she was terrified he was trying to push her away? And that she—terrified and pathetic little mouse that she had become—was afraid to challenge him for fear of what he might say to her?

She injected her voice with all the enthusiasm she

could muster. 'No,' she said cheerfully. 'Nothing's wrong. Why would it be?'

'*Exactly!*' agreed Ursula warmly. 'You're the woman everybody envies—that's the Finn effect! Have a *wonderful* New Year—and I'll see you when I get back.'

'Where are you going?' asked Amber quickly, guilty that she had been so caught up in her own problems she hadn't given a thought to her sister's plans.

'To Prague.'

'And why Prague?'

'Why not?' said Ursula lightly. 'Because it's there, I suppose!'

'Isn't that what someone said when they asked him why he wanted to climb Everest?'

'Clever girl!' Ursula giggled. 'And there was me, hoping to claim it for my own!'

Amber put the phone down and wandered into the sitting room. Only it felt like a hotel, not her home. As if she had no real place in it, and what place she had was only temporary.

Tomorrow was New Year's Eve and they were having a party. No. Correction. *Finn* was having a party. Because she had not been involved in any of the arrangements. Not this year. Last year she had ordered balloons and streamers and the most extravagant chocolate cake that many of the guests had ever seen—or so they had claimed. It had been the first time that he had let her help him, and to Amber it had been a statement to the world of how close they had become.

She remembered the room growing silent as midnight had approached. Finn had got up from the piano and flung open the huge balcony windows, as he always did, and everyone had clustered outside to hear the first mighty boom as Big Ben struck out the first note of the

New Year. Remembered how privileged she had felt to be within earshot of the historic clock.

She had heard it other years, it was true—for Finn had invited her to every party since she had gone to work for him. But last year had been extra special—or rather they had both discovered that their relationship was extra special. Everything had seemed perfect—almost too perfect. They had been living together for almost one blissful year, but Amber had never attempted to define their unspoken harmony to anyone—not even to her sister, for fear of sounding too smug. Or tempting fate.

But harmonious it had been, on just about every level, and Amber had known that—had prayed that she wasn't misreading all the signs. She'd known that she loved him, and had prayed that Finn felt the same way about her. She'd suspected that he did, though he'd never actually said so…at least, not until last year's party…

It had been the usual busy run-up to Christmas, and Amber had been approached to be the face for a big campaign, run by a leading Paris-based company called Cassini. Cassini was an international company and they had been looking for the kind of woman who exemplified all their products—from make-up and perfume to jewellery. A woman who could appeal to *all* their customers, no matter in which country they lived. 'A truly international woman' had been the brief given to Finn and heads of the other major model agencies.

It had been a tall order, and no one had been more surprised than Amber when Cassini had told her that they wanted *her* to be their new face. She rarely modelled, preferring to spend time in the office side by side with Finn, and she hadn't even approached Cassini—it had all happened quite by chance.

The *parfumerie* boss had arrived one day to have lunch with Finn and had seen the slender woman with golden-bright hair wearing faded blue jeans and a white T-shirt, sitting perched on the edge of a desk munching away at an apple.

And, in Finn's own, rather caustic words, the man had been bowled over. 'Smitten.'

'He wants you,' Finn had told her, and Amber had arched her eyebrows delicately.

'Wants me?'

Finn was trying to smile. 'Oh, not in the biblical sense,' he drawled. 'Or, if he does, then he hasn't dared let on to me. No, he wants you to front the new campaign.'

'Oh,' said Amber faintly.

'Surprised?' Finn growled, and she smiled.

'The phrase "knock me down with a feather" springs immediately to mind!'

'It's an exclusive contract. It means mega-mega-bucks,' said Finn. 'Television, magazines, billboards, in-store videos... You'll be made if you accept it, Amber. Financially—if you invest well,' he carried on resolutely, like a man determined to play fair. 'Then you need never work again.'

'And the disadvantages?'

There was a short silence while they stared at one another. He knew exactly what she meant.

'Well, you won't see much of *me*, sugar.'

'Is that a threat?' Amber asked lightly.

He shook his dark head. 'Of course it's not a threat. It's a fact.'

She turned the job down flat. Of course she did. Her life was perfect as it was, and she had everything she needed. Or, rather, she had Finn—and, having got him, she honestly couldn't contemplate life without him.

But, despite having made what she knew was the right

decision, she inevitably felt a little deflated, and was glad that she had Finn's New Year celebration to divert her.

The party that year was bigger than the previous ones she had been to, and Amber kind of got lost in the crush on the balcony. As the first chime pealed out she found she *knew* that Finn's eyes were searching her out. She looked up to find herself locked in that blazing emerald stare, and something previously unacknowledged began to grow to life inside her.

For that gaze touched something buried fathoms deep inside her, a treasure kept hidden for fear that reality would tarnish it and render it useless. In that gaze she recognised that Finn loved her, too—maybe not as much, but love her he did, yes.

Yet...

Was the nagging little insecurity which remained at the base of her heart unique to her—or did all women poised on the brink of love feel it, too?

Why else did she wait with bated breath for Finn to come over to *her* side, so tall and imposing, still wearing black jeans even though most of the other men were in formal dinner suits?

It was at around chime number five, or six—she'd lost count, even when the number to count was so small! He smiled down at her in the sort of melty way she'd often dreamed of.

'Hello,' he said softly.

'Hello,' she said back.

'Have I told you that you look beautiful tonight?'

'No.'

'Well, you do. Very.'

And even though she was surrounded by some of the most exquisite-looking women in London, at that moment, with his green eyes dazzling her, she was secure enough in his feelings for her to smile demurely. 'Why, thank you, Finn.'

He raised her hand slowly to his lips and she guessed that the chimes must nearly be up, though she'd completely lost count by now.

'I love you, Amber O'Neil,' he said, but the way he spoke the words—as if he had just started speaking a foreign language—made her acutely and gratefully aware that he had never said them before. In fact, she very nearly thanked him, but stopped herself just in time!

Afterwards she might despair of the gratitude she felt, but right then she knew only an overwhelming feeling of adoration for him. It was that simple. 'Oh, I love you, too, Finn,' she whispered. 'I love you so much.'

His smile was delighted, but it was the conquering smile of a man who had only received what was due to him. He pulled her properly into his arms then, and kissed her, and when they finally drew apart most people had left the balcony. Amber saw one scrumptious brunette giving them a regretful glance as she departed. Amber had noticed her flirting with Finn all evening, but she hadn't attempted to stop her or to intercede. There was no point playing jealous, not with a man like Finn. He had to be with her for no other reason than because *he* wanted to be.

Now, with the benefit of hindsight, she found herself wondering whether that was why she hadn't taken the Cassini job. Because she didn't think Finn's feelings were strong enough to survive the inevitable absences. That, although she knew he loved her, she suspected that no love could withstand the inevitable temptations which would come *his* way.

So was that really love? How *could* it be love, if she didn't trust him enough to leave him? And maybe Finn was thinking the same thing. Could that be why he had been behaving in a way which was fast becoming hostile?

She felt that she wanted to get away, but there was nowhere to go. Finn was everything to her—not just her love, but her life and her work, too. She had built her whole world around him. She bit her lip as she imagined all the changes she was going to have to make, if it really *was* over.

The telephone cut into her thoughts like a scalpel. It was Finn. He had insisted on going into Allure that morning, saying that he wanted to fiddle around with the computer system before Jackson arrived back from the States.

'Hello, Amber.'

'Hello, Finn.' She waited for the bad news she suspected was coming.

'I'm afraid that I'm going to be late.'

'How late?' asked Amber, frowning.

'Late, late,' he told her obliquely. 'Don't wait up.'

'*That* late? Where are you going?'

There was a pause. 'I'm not going anywhere, honey. I'm staying right here in the office, trying to make some sense out of the chaos. That way, Jackson won't come back to total disarray.'

So why didn't she believe him? Sweat breaking out on her forehead in icy little beads, Amber took a deep breath.

'I might go over to Ursula's.'

'That's nice.' She could hear the faint clicking as he continued to play with his computer as he spoke to her. Didn't he realise how much it infuriated her when he did that?

'I might even stay the night, perhaps.' Amber held her breath, wanting him to demand that she come home, to *his* bed.

'Sounds good,' he told her carefully, and Amber could have wept at the distance which had sprung like some ever-widening chasm between them. 'You could get ready for the party with Ursula, couldn't you? I expect she'd like the company.'

'Ursula isn't coming to the party, Finn, she's made...other plans.' She didn't tell him that Ursula would have already left for Prague. That she would be spending the night alone in her sister's flat. But he was obviously keeping secrets, so why the hell shouldn't she? She made one last conciliatory try. 'I can come back early tomorrow, if you like—and help you get things ready for the party.'

His reply sounded guarded; he didn't sound like Finn at all. 'No need for that, sugar. Everything's organised. I phoned a party-planner to take the hassle out of things.'

Which, she supposed, neatly cut her out of everything. 'Thanks for telling me!' She swallowed down some raw, nameless emotion she didn't dare identify. 'I'll see you tomorrow, then.'

'Yeah.' There was a curious note in his voice. He sounded distant. Detached. Disinterested. 'Bye, Amber.'

'Bye.' She replaced the telephone receiver with a sinking heart, knowing that she could not hide behind platitudes any longer. Their relationship had become a sham and it was sheer cowardice to pretend otherwise.

Well, New Year's Eve was traditionally a night for reflection and the contemplation of change. So be it. Tomorrow night she would pin him down. Tomorrow night she would find out whether Finn still wanted her.

She just couldn't bear to think about what she would say if he didn't...

CHAPTER EIGHT

As SOON as Amber had finished speaking to Finn, she telephoned Ursula, praying that she wouldn't already have left.

'Listen,' she said to her sister, without preamble. 'Can I stay at your place tonight?'

'But I won't be there——'

'I know you won't be there, but I've got a key. Remember?'

'Yes, of course you can stay there.' Ursula sounded puzzled. 'But what exactly——?'

Amber drew in a deep breath. 'Ursula, a few minutes ago you asked me not to question why you were going off to Prague so suddenly. Well, I'm asking you not to question me.'

'Just tell me one thing,' asked her sister urgently. 'Are you okay?'

'Well, I'm not in any danger if that's what you mean, but, no—I'm not okay. Not really.'

'Is this something to do with Finn?'

'What do you think?'

'I think you should talk to him.'

'That's exactly what I'm planning to do.'

'Not run away.' Ursula sounded disapproving now.

Amber sighed. 'I'm not running away. I just need a little space to work out what I want to do. And at the moment he isn't even around for me to talk to. He's out.' And somehow I don't think he's where he says he is. 'Okay?'

'Okay,' said Ursula reluctantly.

Ursula lived on the opposite side of London to Amber and Finn—in Clapham. Her garden flat was tucked away in a quiet road behind the tube station. Amber hadn't been there for ages, and, as she let herself in and dropped her overnight bag in the hall, she reflected that Ursula was sitting on a small goldmine. Her sister was naturally sensible with money; she had saved a deposit and bought a piece of prime real estate in the most recent housing slump—just before prices had rocketed.

Amber looked around the small sitting room. How neat it was. And how tidy. Cushions which had been plumped before Ursula's departure remained plumped— there would be no indentation of a man's head there, where he had sprawled out on a sofa reading a book. No desert boots kicked into a sandy heap in the corner. Amber swallowed, knowing that staying here tonight was more than a need to escape and a chance to get her thoughts in order.

Because tonight was a practice run. If, in her worst-case scenario, she *was* to split up with Finn, then she would soon be living alone in a flat like this.

Or, rather, she wouldn't. She would be at a disadvantage—starting from scratch in her mid-twenties. She wouldn't be able to afford a shoebox in *this* area—and she was damned if she was going to ask Finn for any kind of maintenance.

She wandered into the bedroom and stared at Ursula's pristine and neatly tucked bed; she found herself wondering whether there had ever been a man in that bed. Ursula would never scatter crumbs in the sheets, that was for sure.

Amber sighed as she wandered into the kitchen, her vision of the future bleak as she imagined a tiny bedsit in a grotty part of the city, with the loud music of neighbours blaring out all night. She didn't even dare think about finding a new job.

But then she thought of her mother, and the *real* hardship which she had been forced to endure—all the poverty and loneliness of bringing two children up on her own. So what were her own problems in comparison? She loved Finn with a fervour which sometimes startled her—but if the relationship was coming to an end, then so be it. She certainly wasn't going to *beg* him not to finish it. Women had been surviving and coping with broken love affairs for generations. And she was known and respected by the other leading model agencies in London—there would always be a job as a booker *somewhere*.

She must be *strong*. She owed it to herself. And if tomorrow night was going to be the final scene in her relationship, then she was going to exit the stage with a dramatic flourish.

She would dress to kill—she would use every trick in the book, plus a few more, and somehow she would outshine the beautiful women who would no doubt be circling him as hungrily as piranha fish, scenting that his relationship was on the rocks.

She was going to show Finn Fitzgerald *exactly* what he was going to be missing!

Finn's New Year party always started at nine-thirty— late enough to make people hungry to be there. Or so he said. Amber suspected that people would be eager to be there if the entire proceedings lasted just five minutes!

She planned to be late, but it was a task more difficult than she had anticipated. It *was* a long time to wait— especially when you had nothing in particular planned. And the last day of the year had such a strange feel to it. People walked around either looking glum or mani-

acally happy—depending on how their year had been.
Amber spent a great part of the morning perfecting a
devil-may-care expression in the mirror.

She hadn't spent so long getting ready since the very
first time that Finn had taken her out—to a tiny, dark
restaurant where her dress had been indistinguishable in
the subdued lighting, and later he had peeled the garment
from her body with her scarcely even noticing it!

Well, he certainly wouldn't be peeling the dress from
her body tonight, she thought grimly. Not unless he
came crawling to her with sincere apologies and some
kind of explanation for the miserable way he had been
behaving lately!

She spent the afternoon shopping, finally finding the
ideal, unforgettable dress—an outrageous slip of a thing
in turquoise silk-satin which made her eyes look even
bluer. It was shorter than she usually wore, moulding
her breasts and bottom like a second skin, and the flirty,
strappy high-heeled sandals she bought to accompany it
made her legs look as if they went on forever. With her
hair dried into a syrup-shiny fall—and more make-up
than she had *ever* worn—she felt ready to face Finn with
something approaching equanimity.

But as she took the lift up to the flat at twenty minutes
past eleven, she found that her confidence seemed to be
ebbing away.

She rang the doorbell, having decided that the impact
of her arrival would be lost if she simply let herself in,
and the door was pulled open almost immediately by
Finn himself, who looked like a study in dark, simmer-
ing rage. He was dressed entirely in black—the only
colour relief was the watchful glitter of his eyes, which
looked almost unnaturally green against the pallor of his
face. His body language was uncompromising—tough
and uncompromising—and yet his strong, sexual mag-

netism surrounded him like an aura. He looked edgy, too.

'Where have you been?' he demanded.

'But you know where I've been. At Ursula's.'

He sent an exaggerated and glowering look of disbelief at his wristwatch. 'Until *this* time?'

Amber felt like smirking, but decided against it. She had never *seen* him so angry before. Maybe this was the kind of behaviour to which Finn responded best. Maybe in the past she had been too sweetly compliant. 'Actually, no,' she told him evenly. 'I've been prowling round the red-light district in Soho, looking for customers!'

With slow deliberation, he let his eyes travel from the tip of her head to the tip of her toes, and something in that candid, sexual scrutiny made her blush and tingle like a seventeen-year-old. 'Well, you're certainly dressed for it,' he drawled insultingly.

She felt like slapping him—well, actually, she felt like doing something else to him, much to her disgust. But both options were out. This was a party. And she was going to behave with dignity...

'Aren't you going to invite me in?'

'Since when did you need an invitation?' But he stood aside to let her pass, and as she deliberately brushed against him she heard his ragged inhalation of breath. She found that she was holding her own breath, wondering whether he would touch her. Pull her into his arms. Kiss her. Or drag her straight off to bed and damn the party.

But he did none of those things.

Instead, his eyes were riveted to the blue silk-satin which skimmed her bottom. 'Are you wearing any knickers under that dress?' he demanded hotly.

'Wouldn't you like to know?' she asked him, her serene manner belying the rattling pace of her heart as she set off in search of a drink she had never needed so badly in her life.

Finn followed her across the room, yet she could almost *sense* his reluctance to do so—as though he was being drawn towards her against his will. She watched the women who eyed him so greedily, but for now, at least, his attention was solely on *her*. For the first time ever in their relationship, she felt suffused with a heady knowledge of her sexual power over him.

But her hand was shaking as she took a glass of champagne from a passing waitress. She drank it down in one and put the empty glass on a table, before turning to look around the room. Amber was glad she had opted for the turquoise dress, since, as usual—it being a London party—every woman in the room was wearing black. Anyone visiting from another country would be forgiven for thinking that they had walked into a funeral by mistake, she thought wryly. Though, with this gloomy air of foreboding sitting on her shoulders like a heavy mantle, it *felt* a bit like a funeral. Amber looked around for something else to drink.

'Are you planning to get drunk?' came a familiar baritone from behind her. She turned round to find Finn standing there, all broody, sensual menace—and his presence affected her far more than the hastily drunk champagne had done.

She met his accusing stare head-on. 'I might be.'

'Why?'

'Need you ask?' Amber turned on him, suddenly sick of all this game-playing, the unknown twists and turns which their relationship seemed to be taking. The fact that he could be some icy and distant stranger, instead of her warm, loving Finn. She had planned to wait until midnight, but suddenly she couldn't contemplate waiting a second longer. It was crunch time. 'You've been evasive and bad-tempered and acting oddly for days now—and please don't insult my intelligence by trying to deny it!' She noticed that he didn't. 'So are you trying in some not-very-subtle way to tell me something, Finn?'

His eyes grew wary, the thick lashes acting like shades so that she could only make out a watchful glimmer of green. 'And what would I be trying to tell you, Amber?'

'I don't *know*!' She grew exasperated now. 'That's why I'm asking! You've been *unbearable* to live with—there's no other word to describe it—completely *unbearable*! I don't know what I'm supposed to have done, or not done—apart, of course—' and her voice rose '—from the heinous crime of scattering crumbs all over the damned bed! Or daring to tell some magazine our innocent little story—'

'Amber—'

'Don't *Amber* me!' she ground out from between gritted teeth, not caring that they could be overheard, or that people were looking, or that—oh, *hell*—Karolina Lindberg and her glamorous mother had just come in, and were busy scanning the room, presumably looking for Finn. But he didn't appear to notice—his attention was totally on her as she shook her mane of golden hair with frustration. 'Stop sending me out such mixed messages and give me a clear explanation of what is happening,' she whispered. 'That's all I ask.'

'For God's sake, Amber,' said Finn, in a voice which sounded like a broken plea. 'Why do you have to make this so hard for me? Why did you have to look so damned gorgeous tonight?'

All Amber could see was that Finn's eyes were riveted to the swell of her silk-covered breasts. She nodded in comprehension as an odd, kicking sense of disappointment stabbed through her. '*Oh!* I think I get it,' she said slowly. 'Clearly I'm nothing but a body to you these

days. Someone who you still desire but no longer respect, although, now I come to think of it, you haven't
expressed much desire for *me* lately, have you, Finn?
And there's only one believable explanation as to why
that might be—'

'Hello, Finn!' An attractively low voice broke into
their conversation, and Amber and Finn both looked up
to find Karolina's mother, Birgitta, standing there—with
her striking but sulky-looking daughter at her side.

Unable to stop herself, Amber glared at the two
women, but especially at Birgitta. Couldn't she see that
they didn't want to be interrupted? That they were having an intense conversation which most people with even
a *tiny* bit of perception could tell was a private conversation?

With her sexy Swedish accent, Birgitta pronounced
the word 'Feen'. Pretty irresistible, judging from the
smile on 'Feen's' face—which was warmer than any
smile he had given *her* so far this evening!

'I'm told that you will be playing the piano later,' said
Birgitta prettily, as she flicked a strand of white-blonde
hair back off her shoulder. 'I cannot wait to hear it! I
gather that you are a very talented man!'

Amber saw Finn tense up, and her eyes narrowed. He
never suffered from nerves about playing. So why was
he so jumpy? Because of the situation he found himself
in, perhaps. She watched Birgitta smiling up at him with
a look of sheer adoration.

And Finn didn't look away...

Amber's heart pounded in her chest and she felt dizzy
with a cloying, choking fear. She had been jealous of all
the attention which Finn had paid to Birgitta, sure—but
it had been his *time* she had coveted, nothing more. She
had never imagined for a moment that there might be
anything more in it than that. And yet...Birgitta was

about thirty-five, just a little older than Finn, and no one cared about age differences like that any more—not these days. Surely…surely…

Was that what he had been trying to tell her? Why his attitude had changed so remarkably these past weeks?

He seemed to remember that she was there. 'Amber—you remember Birgitta, don't you?'

'How could I ever forget?' Amber gave the ghost of a smile, but she knew she had to get away from them before she made a fool of herself in front of fifty New Year revellers. 'Will you excuse me for a moment?' she said hurriedly, and made her way through the guests, not daring to meet all the curious eyes which followed her. Wondering if her face showed her distress.

In the bathroom she realised that it did. She stood looking at her wild-eyed reflection in the mirror, at the way her chest heaved as she fought for breath and sanity. On one of the glass shelves stood *her* bottles of bath essence and body lotion. The perfumed bath oil which Ursula had bought as one of her Christmas presents.

And sitting sadly neglected by the empty bath were three plastic yellow ducks, bought as a joke present by Finn when she had first gone to work with him. She had treasured those cheap little ducks almost as much as the diamond ring he had put on her finger. Maybe more. With the ring had come nothing but trouble—and the niggling fear that getting engaged had been a huge mistake.

But she would never know unless she asked Finn.

The temptation to run away was overwhelming, but she fought it, and relief mingled with panic when she heard someone knocking at the bathroom door. She knew from the authoritative thumping just who it was, even before she heard Finn's voice call out her name.

She flung the door open and looked at him.

'Amber.' He spoke her name as if it was an ending.

'Amber, what?' Her voice was very low. 'Amber, I'm sorry I've been so distracted? Amber, you mustn't mind when I foist so much attention on the beautiful mother of one of my models?'

'You're making this very difficult for me, you know,' he said softly.

'What's difficult? If you don't love me any more, Finn, then all you have to do is come out and tell me.'

'And what if I told you that it isn't that easy?'

She froze. She had been gambling on complete denial, not that uncomfortable expression on his face, as though he had some terrible secret...

'Finn!' called a voice from along the corridor, and Amber could have wept with frustration.

'Dear heaven!' she exclaimed. 'Can't we have a private conversation around here?'

'Maybe if you hadn't chosen not to turn up earlier, before the place was packed with people, then we might have been able to achieve it!' he bit out.

'And maybe if *you* hadn't been so darned uncommunicative lately, then I wouldn't have chosen so unwisely!' she stormed back. 'You couldn't *wait* to pack me off to Ursula's! You made it perfectly clear that you didn't want my help. That this was *your* party! And you cut me out of it as surely as you've cut me out of every other section of your life just lately!' She paused for breath, just as Finn's accountant, Andy, appeared round the corner.

'Oh, hell!' He squirmed awkwardly. 'From the expressions on your faces—seems like I've chosen a bad time.'

'The worst possible,' agreed Finn, with a half-smile.

'But I'm sure that whatever you have to say won't take long. What is it, Andy?'

'Just that it's getting on for midnight, and they're all waiting for you to play.'

'Make sure everyone has charged their glasses, and tell them I'll be along in a moment,' Finn promised.

'Okay! Can do!' said Andy, and beat a hasty retreat.

They watched him go in silence, and then Finn turned to look at her, his face full of regret, and of something else too—something which Amber wasn't used to seeing there. Because, right then, he looked almost *vulnerable*. And, even in the midst of all her anger and confusion, Amber found herself wanting to comfort him, to put her arms around him and soothe the unhappiness from his face.

'I've been trying to talk to you for days.' He sighed. 'Only the time never seems right.'

'Or maybe you keep putting it off?' she guessed.

'Yeah, maybe I do—you're too perceptive,' he observed, but the gentle mockery didn't quite ring true.

Her anger evaporated as she found herself reaching up to touch his face, and the caress of her fingers on his skin felt somehow alien to her. She quickly realised why. It had been so *long* since she had touched him.

'Something's wrong, Finn,' she whispered. 'Something has been wrong for days now, and I don't know what it is and, unless you tell me, then we can't work it out.' She heard the familiar opening chord of that year's best-selling Christmas record, and could have screamed with frustration. 'But now is clearly not the right time. So let's go into the party and we'll pretend we're a happy couple. You play your piece, and then we'll see the New Year in, just like we always do. And afterwards, when everyone has gone, then we'll sit down and sort it out, whatever it is.'

'God, you're so sure of yourself, Amber.' His eyes flicked over her with admiration. 'So certain that everything can be patched up and made perfect, aren't you?'

'Not perfect,' she told him quietly, her eyes searching his face for clues, but it gave nothing away. 'Because nothing ever is. But something better than what we've had just lately.'

'That shouldn't be too difficult,' he mocked.

She sucked in an agonised breath, knowing that she was gambling every bit of pride she possessed with her next statement. But what was pride if it meant a lifetime without the man she wanted? 'I love you, Finn,' she told him simply. 'I always have done—and that's the bottom line. But if you don't feel the same way about me any more, then all you have to do is tell me. And I'll go. Because I can cope with anything you throw at me.' She paused for a moment. 'Except that.'

'*Finn!*' called out an impatient voice from the sitting room.

He looked down into her upturned face and she was shocked at the tension lines which had deepened the grooves running down the side of his mouth. 'I could tell them all to go to hell,' he reflected, but for once his voice lacked conviction.

'Humour them,' she said urgently, alarmed at the passive acceptance in his voice, which was not like Finn at all... 'Humour them until we're alone.'

He seemed about to say something, but must have changed his mind because he briefly closed his eyes, then squared his shoulders and began to walk towards the sitting room like a man to his execution, with Amber at his side.

'Hey, Finn!' called someone. 'Ready to boogie?'

But he didn't answer, just walked through the waiting party-goers who parted to clear a path to the piano.

Amber nodded and said hello to several people, though afterwards she didn't have a clue whom she had spoken to. But then her attention was really all on Finn. She fixed a smile onto her lips as she watched him sit down, but thought how jerky his movements were as he positioned his legs beneath the piano.

Her smile didn't slip for a moment, not even when Birgitta, in a sequin-bright dress, draped herself over the piano and stood gazing at him, starstruck. Meanwhile Karolina was looking bored and shovelling popcorn into her mouth, looking—for once—not a day older than her sixteen years.

Silence filled the room as Finn lifted his hands to begin, but seemed to hesitate. Amber frowned slightly as she saw his fingers tremble before clenching into whitened fists over the keyboard.

Then he suddenly rose to his feet, and very deliberately, almost unsteadily, he pulled Birgitta away from the piano and into his arms. Birgitta stared up at him, her pale eyes startled but compliant, her mouth pouting towards him in naked invitation. And that was when Finn started kissing her, to the shocked gasps of those watching.

Then the faces all turned as one towards Amber, and it was the last thing she saw—those curious eyes, those shocked and disbelieving expressions.

The image branded itself onto her mind like her very worst nightmare, before she turned on her heels and ran out of the flat just as fast as her feet would carry her.

CHAPTER NINE

Two things happened in the week which followed Finn's party. The first was the entirely predictable newspaper coverage of what had happened that night, and, since Amber was already feeling miserable and a fool, she was immune to its salacious content. But the second rocked the very foundations of her world.

After Finn's very public kiss with Birgitta, Amber had run outside and caught a taxi straight to Ursula's flat, where, once inside the door, she had collapsed and sobbed like a hunted animal.

Except that no one was hunting her. That much soon became clear by the silence which ticked on through the night into one of the most miserable dawns she could remember.

She *could* have disconnected the telephone, telling herself that she had no desire to speak to Finn, and that he would know exactly where she was staying. But she *didn't* disconnect it—and then felt doubly stupid when it mocked her with its deafening silence.

She didn't sleep a wink—she couldn't—her mind was too busy torturing her with images of what must have happened after she had gone. Because kisses like that between two consenting adults had only one conclusion. Adults didn't kiss and then say goodnight. Amber shuddered as she imagined Finn naked and coupled with Birgitta—his dark honeyed skin contrasting so magnificently against her icy, Nordic beauty as he drove his sweet, hard flesh into her...

Amber got up and staggered over to the sink to retch yet again, but her stomach was aching and empty.

She spent the following day in a daze, too disorientated to contemplate leaving the flat—and besides, it was a bank holiday. She couldn't face seeing the carefree faces of people out enjoying themselves—she felt that her own unhappiness would blight other people's enjoyment.

That evening, she took a hot bath and then drank two huge glasses of wine—and the combination of liquor and utter fatigue was enough to ensure that she spent the night dead to the world.

She awoke to the sound of the newspapers being delivered. Ursula always ordered two—a hefty broadsheet for 'proper' news, and one of the better tabloids just for fun.

With trembling fingers, Amber fumbled through the pages of the *Daily View*, until she had reached Janet Jenson's notoriously popular gossip column. And there it was. In black and white. Newsprint made it real. And tacky.

FINN WON'T CATWALK DOWN THE AISLE!

Amber's first irreverent thought was how much he would hate the headline—he loathed references to his former life as a male model! She read on.

Hunky Finn Fitzgerald, millionaire owner of London's leading agency, Allure, has split with the lovely Amber O'Neil—just weeks after she gave an exclusive interview to *Wow!* magazine about their recent engagement!

Finn, who has been squiring the flame-haired Amber for almost two years, chose to end the relationship with a suitably dramatic flourish at his annual New Year's party. He was last seen smooching on top

of a grand piano, with the mother of sensational new
Allure model, Karolina Lindberg.

Amber is not only engaged to Finn, she also works
for him at Allure—so the New Year should see
fireworks in their exclusive corner of London!

Screwing the newspaper up with a howl of disgust,
Amber threw herself down on the sofa, and sobbed.

Two days later, she was sitting disconsolately staring
into space when she heard the sound of a key being
turned in the front door and she looked up in alarm to
see Ursula struggling over the doorstep, carrying a small
suitcase and overnight bag.

Ursula dropped the bags as if they were stones. She
didn't look like herself at all—her normal rosy face was
deathly pale and her mouth thin and unsmiling.

'Oh, Amber,' she moaned. 'I'm so very sorry.'

Amber laid her head in her arms and burst into re-
newed tears.

Ursula let her cry, just bustled around the kitchen
making tea and toast in her big-sister way, just as she
had when they'd been teenagers and their mother had
been so ill.

It wasn't until she had pushed a steaming mug and a
slice of hot buttered toast towards Amber that she said,
in a voice raw with sorrow, 'I couldn't believe it when
I read about it in the newspapers! And even then I *still*
didn't believe it!'

Amber sniffed. 'I could hardly believe it myself—but
I actually had to witness it!'

'Of course.' Ursula patted her sister's arm, her face
distorted with concern. 'It must have been terrible for
you.'

'Terrible?' Amber gave a hollow laugh. 'I'll say it was

terrible—my whole world came crashing down around my ears!'

'Well, it may not be as bad as you imagine,' Ursula soothed. 'There surely is *some* hope?'

Amber stared at her sister askance. 'Do you really think I'd have him back after *that*?'

Ursula's mouth briefly tightened. 'I hope you don't mean that, Amber.'

Amber's eyes widened. 'You aren't serious?'

'Of course I'm serious!' said Ursula crossly. 'I didn't have you down for a coward, Amber O'Neil!'

'Coward?' It was a relief to feel something other than hurt and humiliation, and righteous anger flooded through Amber's veins like a powerful drug. 'If anyone's the coward—it's Finn! Why the hell didn't he have the guts to tell me?'

'Because he's a big, strong, powerful man, and men like that find it difficult to—'

'Tie themselves down to one woman?' put in Amber caustically. 'You mean they're so big and powerful that they have to screw anything that moves!'

'Amber O'Neil! I never thought I'd live to hear you talk like that!'

'Well, I *feel* like using bad language! It's better than getting blind drunk or going round and smashing up his so-called luxury apartment—which are the other two options!'

'Amber,' said Ursula gently, 'Finn's a sick man.'

'You're telling me he's sick!'

'And he needs your support right now.'

Amber nearly fell off her chair. 'You can't mean that, Ursula,' she said slowly.

'Oh, but I do.'

'Let me get this straight…' Amber fixed her eyebrows together in a frown. 'You expect me to welcome Finn back—even supposing he wanted to come—after he's been unfaithful to me?'

Ursula almost dropped the teapot. She put it down on the tray with a shaking hand. 'Finn's been *unfaithful*?' she queried incredulously. 'To *you*?'

'Well, of course he has! What do you think we've been talking about? Why do you think I'm still here— with eyes which look like pincushions? Finn and I split up on New Year's Eve after he virtually made love to one of the models' mothers all over the top of his grand piano!'

But her words did not have the effect on Ursula that she would have imagined. Instead, her sister looked even more worried. 'You mean you haven't heard?'

'Heard what? Don't tell me that they've rushed off and got married? I didn't think she was even divorced!'

Ursula swallowed. She had once had to tell Amber that their mother was very sick; this now seemed almost as bad.

'Amber, I want you to listen to me very carefully,' she said, in a low voice. 'Finn is very ill. Very ill indeed. He's in hospital. He's paralysed—'

'Paralysed?' Amber repeated the word in disbelief, because surely Ursula must have made a mistake. The world swayed, then righted itself again.

'I'm so very sorry,' said Ursula gently.

'No!' Amber shouted in denial. Dots danced in front of her eyes and a great muffling roar rose up and constricted her ears as she felt herself slipping forward...

When she opened her eyes, she had her head bent over her knees, with Ursula smoothing her hair back from a cold and clammy neck. She tried to sit up, but Ursula wouldn't let her.

'I thought you knew!'

Amber shook her head muzzily. 'Knew what? Will you please tell me what is going on?'

Ursula helped her over to the sofa. 'Ross read about it in Prague—it's been all over the news. Finn is desperately ill with some bizarre illness called...' she frowned with concentration as she tried to remember how to pronounce it '...Guillain-Barré syndrome. He was rushed into hospital—'

'Which hospital, Ursula?' demanded Amber urgently. '*Which* hospital?'

'St Jude's.'

'Just call me a cab,' said Amber grimly. 'I must go to him.'

'Now?'

'This very minute!'

'Then I'm coming with you!'

The journey to St Jude's seemed to take for ever, and the taxi seemed interminably slow as it crawled its way through the London traffic. Amber was scarcely aware of her surroundings—in fact she barely noticed a word of what her sister was saying to her. She had wanted to come on her own, but Ursula had insisted on accompanying her, telling her that she was too vulnerable in her present state to be left on her own.

Vulnerable?

She wasn't the one who was vulnerable. Her beloved Finn was the vulnerable one, lying sick in some lonely hospital bed. She gulped down the ever-present sob which seemed to have taken up residence in the back of her throat and blindly walked into the reception area of St Jude's, where people instinctively stepped aside to let her pass, their faces frightened as they looked into her haunted eyes.

A silent metallic lift sped up to the intensive care unit, and Amber couldn't help but notice the alarm on the face of the charge-nurse sitting at the nurses' station and writing in the notes as she half stumbled towards him. Her arms and legs seemed to be on some uncoordinated automatic pilot; her limbs didn't seem to belong to *her* any more.

She found herself briefly wondering what kind of spectacle she must present—her eyes wild with grief and red with weeping. She had dressed in the first things that had come to her shaking fingers—everything was mismatched—and she had done little more than drag a brush through the tangle of her hair. But she didn't care. She didn't care about anything except seeing Finn.

The charge-nurse rose to his feet. 'Can I help you?'

'Where's Finn?' Amber blurted out.

A professional look of concern came over his face. 'Perhaps you would like to—'

'I want to see Finn Fitzgerald! *Please!*' she begged.

'And you are?'

'I'm his—' Amber waved her left hand in front of the man's face to show him her sparkling diamond, as if to validate her words, but then she remembered that she had taken it off. Torn it from her finger and stuffed it to the back of a drawer as soon as she had arrived at Ursula's, having run away from the public humiliation of seeing him kissing another woman.

But suddenly that seemed of no consequence. How could she care about *that*—about *anything*—when Finn was lying, fighting for his life? Her darling, beloved Finn.

'I'm his fiancée,' she said weakly. 'I'm Amber O'Neil and I must see him. I *must*!'

The charge-nurse frowned. 'I'm afraid that his family are with him at the moment, and there have to be limits about the amount of visitors he's allowed to have—'

'Well, how *is* he, for heaven's sake? You must be able to tell me *that*!'

The charge-nurse shook his head. 'You must understand that we've had a number of requests about Mr Fitzgerald's condition,' he answered gently. 'The press have been swarming around the place like locusts, and we can't just give out information without checking. So if you'd like to take a seat—'

Amber only just stopped herself from grabbing the charge-nurse by his lapels and shaking him. She must calm down. The man was only doing his job—and she was in such a state that she probably didn't look *fit* to see a sick person.

She drew a deep, soothing breath. 'Have his family flown over from Ireland?'

'Yes, I believe they have.'

'Then please go and check with them,' said Amber, trying to get the words out in a steady voice. 'They'll vouch for me. They'll tell you I'm who I say I am. And he'll want to see me!'

The charge-nurse nodded and disappeared, returning minutes later with Finn's sister Philomena at his side. The oldest of the seven Fitzgerald offspring, Philomena had met Amber just the once, when Finn had taken her to Ireland for Easter last year. Philomena was almost fifty, now a grandmother herself, and normally the most unflappable of women, but right now her face looked as white and as fragile as parchment.

'My dear child,' she moaned, and put her arms tight round Amber. 'Dear, dear child. What in the name of God has been happening?'

Amber *felt* like a child, clasped in Philomena's firm grip—she would have liked to have stayed like that all day if it hadn't been for the grim reality of what was happening. 'H-how is he?'

'He's a sick man, Amber,' said Philomena quietly. 'Very sick indeed. He can't breathe for himself—he's on a ventilator.'

'Dear God!' gasped Amber, as if she had been punched.

Philomena closed her eyes in despair, but ploughed on with the stark, horrible truth. 'He's paralysed in all four limbs, and they don't know what the outcome might be. He's a strong man—the doctors say he's as strong as an ox—but there's no telling—'

'Excuse me?'

As if in a daze, Philomena dropped her arms at the sound of a low, foreign accent, and Amber couldn't believe the evidence of her own eyes as she looked up to see Birgitta crossing the shiny floor towards them. She froze with outrage and shock. How dared she? How *dared* she show her face here?

Ridiculously, and obsessively, Amber noticed the Swedish woman's clothes. She was wearing a pristine ice-pink suit—so that today she did not resemble a *femme fatale* at all, but instead looked like some sleek, efficient air hostess. How could she? thought Amber brokenly. How could she put her make-up on so neatly and co-ordinate all her clothes when Finn was lying close to death?

Instinct powered over restraint, and Amber turned on the woman, her eyes blazing, her fists clenched tightly by her side. 'What are you doing here, Birgitta?'

Birgitta's mouth flattened. 'I was asked to come.'

'Really?' questioned Amber. 'I find that a little difficult to believe!'

'But—'

'How have you got the *nerve* to turn up here, after everything you've done? Is that how you get by in life?

By publicly throwing yourself at other women's fiancés?'

Birgitta's eyes widened in surprise. 'But Finn kissed *me*,' she pointed out. 'Don't you remember?'

Philomena placed a confining hand on Amber's arm, but Amber took no notice. 'He doesn't *want* you here, Birgitta!' she spat. 'He's sick and he's *mine*! So get *out*!'

Was that regret or apology which briefly appeared in Birgitta's ice-blue eyes? she wondered. 'Amber, it's *you* I want to speak to—'

'Well, tough! I'm busy and I've got nothing that I want to say to you! Do you understand? *Nothing*—other than to ask you to leave. Right *now*!'

With an expression of regret, the Swedish woman reached into her ice-pink handbag and pulled out an envelope. As soon as Amber saw the distinctive, sloping black handwriting, she didn't need to ask whose hand had written it.

'Feen asked me to give you this.'

Some deep, unfurling fear made Amber want to reject the letter, but she couldn't do that—especially not now, when Finn was so ill. She snatched the envelope from Birgitta's pale fingers and carried it over to the corner of the room, her own hands shaking like crazy. She stood by the visitors' coffee machine while she ripped the envelope open to read it.

It was not Finn's usual flowing and fluid style—it was a short and somewhat stilted note, and she wondered how difficult it must have been for him to write. Not half as difficult as it was for her to read, she would wager.

It had been written on New Year's Day, and it said,

Dear Amber,
I know I have chosen a cowardly way to go about

telling you, but I fear that I can no longer see a future together for us. As you will no doubt have judged from my recent behaviour, I have grown extremely fond of Birgitta—and you know that I have always been a one-woman man. You have meant a great deal to me, and you always will. We shared so many good things, and I would rather leave the memories of all those times intact. Therefore, I think it best if we did not see each other again, at least for the time being.

Yours ever, Finn.

There was, Amber noted dully, no mention of love. She turned round to see Philomena standing watching. Finn's sister was clearly confused by events—but it was Birgitta's beautiful, serene face which scorched its way indelibly into her line of vision, like a mocking, triumphant symbol of everything she had lost.

Holding the note aloft, like a white flag of surrender, Amber met Birgitta's eyes. 'Do you know what the note says?' she demanded, her voice sounding reedy. '*Do* you?'

Birgitta nodded. 'He showed it to me, yes.'

'And he's in love with you? Or thinks he is?'

Birgitta gave a wry smile. She appeared to choose her words very carefully, and when she spoke she sounded extremely formal, and yet—conversely—more foreign than ever before. 'I would not presume to talk of love at this stage. We have not known each other for long enough.'

From out of the corner of her eye, Amber could see that Ursula had appeared by Philomena's side, and was watching her warily, as if afraid of what she would do next.

Well, what *would* she do next? Launch herself at

Birgitta? Punch? Kick? Scream? Shout? Cry? Maybe all of these?

And lose what little dignity she had left?

Amber turned to Philomena, her face full of appeal. 'Please, can I see him—just for a moment?'

Philomena flushed, her face uncomfortable. She looked at Ursula, and an almost imperceptible shake of the head passed between the two women. 'I think perhaps it's better that you don't—'

Amber looked at Birgitta, and swallowed down the primitive desire to pull her flaxen hair out by the roots. Instead she took a step forward, but, to her credit, Birgitta did not flinch.

'Just you make sure you look after him properly!' Amber warned, her voice in danger of cracking in defeat.

But then some innate pride—inspired by the love she knew she and Finn *had* shared—came flooding over her like a soothing balm.

For he had once loved her enough to put his ring on her finger and want to marry her, and now he lay poised between life and death. She would not run out of there like some vanquished loser.

Instead, she nodded almost regally to her sister, and she and Ursula walked out of the unit, side by side.

They did not speak to each other all the way down in the lift, nor even in the taxi, which Amber directed to Finn's apartment. She was too fraught and too terrified of breaking down to be able to utter a single word, and one look at her sister was enough to keep Ursula silent for the rest of the journey.

It felt like a lifetime since Amber had been at the flat. There was still some debris left over from the party, and some lingering remnant of domesticity almost had her loading up the dishwasher, until she remembered her situation and stopped. No doubt Birgitta would be coming back here to tidy things away. She turned to her sister instead, her face deathly pale and oddly calm.

'Will you wait while I pack up a few things?'

'Of course I will.'

'And can I store them at your flat?'

'Oh, Amber! Of course you can! You can stay there for as long as you like—you know that.'

But Amber shook her head regretfully. 'No, I can't do that. I'll stay—but only for as long as it takes to find out if Finn will be...' She swallowed back the words, as if saying them would make them real. 'Until I know that Finn's out of danger.'

'And what will you do after that?'

Amber stared sightlessly around the bright flat which had once been her home. 'I don't know.'

CHAPTER TEN

OUTSIDE, the morning sky was the palest powder-blue, expensively gilded with gold, and Amber dunked her croissant into the bowl of milky coffee and ate with an appetite which was gradually returning to normal.

Odd, really—she felt as though she were convalescing from some terrible, debilitating illness. Though maybe she was—hadn't people in the Middle Ages considered love to be like a sickness?

Still, she must put that love behind her now. It was all over. There had been a total news blackout on Finn's progress, but, according to a sweet letter sent by Philomena, he was 'recovering slowly'. As soon as she had received it, Amber had taken herself off to the South of France for her own kind of recovery.

Not the warmest place to be in spring, true, but an infinitely better place to be than London, where the memories of the man she couldn't seem to stop loving were still too acute to be bearable. Everyone told her that *of course* you recovered from a broken heart, that it was a necessary part of your emotional development to go through a bust-up, and that you came out of it on the other side a stronger person all round.

And Amber believed them. She wanted to believe them. She had to. It was the one thing she was clinging onto: that one day this terrible black cloud of missing him would lift from over her. Next week she would begin to plan her future—a future which she suspected would keep her well clear of the fish-bowl world of modelling...

'Mademoiselle?'

Amber looked up. Monsieur Joseph was the patron of the hotel Plan-du-Var, where she had gone after finding out that Finn *would* get better. Ursula's boss, Ross Sheridan, had recommended the small and simple *pension* which lay by the side of the river Var, up in the mountains above Nice. There were few guests staying in the tiny village of Plan-du-Var at this time of year, and Monsieur Joseph and his family had welcomed her as if she had been one of their own.

In the three months since she had been there, Amber had done little more than rest, read and take walks through the breathtaking countryside. And Jackson had flown back to England just as soon as he had heard about Finn's illness, so at least she knew that Allure was safe in his capable hands. Though why she still cared about Allure...

'Mademoiselle?' Amber looked up as Monsieur Joseph prompted her once more. *'C'est le téléphone!'*

'Merci, Monsieur.' Amber went through into the private *salon* and picked up the phone.

'Allô!' she said automatically.

'Amber, it's Ursula!'

Fine beads of sweat misted Amber's forehead. 'Is it Finn?'

'In a word, yes.'

'He hasn't relapsed?'

'No.' There was a pause. 'I'm acting as a go-between, Amber.'

'How do you mean?'

'Finn has asked me to set up a meeting between you and him.'

'Why?'

'He wouldn't...didn't say. He just wants you to agree to meet him.'

Amber gave a feigned laugh. 'He doesn't want *much*, does he? Why doesn't he ask me himself?'

There was silence at the other end of the phone. 'How are you, Amber?'

'I'm fine. Well, fine-*ish*.' She sighed. 'I don't want to talk about how *I* am—how's Finn?'

'I haven't seen him. He's only just rung and asked me to arrange a meeting.'

'So everything is to be on Finn's terms, huh?'

'Do you want me to tell him no?'

Amber snorted. 'Of course I don't want you to tell him no! I *have* to see him.'

'Amber—' Ursula's voice sounded worried. 'Are you still as much in love with him as before?'

'What kind of a question is that?'

Ursula sighed. 'A sisterly question. A concerned question. Are you?'

'I'm not a victim, Ursula. I don't hanker after men who make it plain they don't want me.'

'So you're not?'

'I *do* want to see him,' said Amber, realising that she hadn't answered Ursula's question, and realising that she wasn't going to. It was too shameful to admit that she still cared, but of *course* she still cared. True love was something that grew—and her love had been true, even if Finn's had not. And it didn't just wither and die overnight. That took time. And effort.

She tried to explain her feelings to her sister. 'I need to see Finn, to see him as a real person again. At the moment, he's all these conflicting romantic images in my mind—the dream lover and the philandering bastard who then lies critically ill on his sickbed. I need to see Finn *now*. Post-illness—and post-*me*. I need to see him as some *other* woman's dream lover, no longer mine.'

'You're not saying that you want him to bring *Birgitta* with him?' Ursula's voice sounded outraged.

Amber swallowed down the bitter bile of jealousy. 'Of course I don't. I don't need to see her with him to know that he's no longer mine. I've had time enough to get used to that fact. So, yes, Ursula—I'll see him. In England, I presume?'

'I'll find out. He didn't give me any details, just wanted me to find out whether you would agree to see him in principle.'

'Tell him I'll look forward to it,' said Amber grittily.

'Well, I've some slightly more cheerful news for you, too! You remember Mother's wedding dress?'

Amber winced, glad that her sister couldn't see her, but thinking all the same that it really wasn't the most diplomatic of subjects to be bringing up right now. 'Yes,' she answered calmly, wondering what this could possibly have to do with anything.

'And you remember me telling you about the woman whose mother designed the dress? The one who owns the wedding shop—Holly Lovelace?'

Amber tried to clear her mind of the dominating images of Finn, which had spread like tentacles into every conscious thought. 'Er, yes,' she said vaguely, trying to recall an evening when life had been normal. A long time ago, it seemed now. 'I think so. Why?'

'Well, her fiancé, Luke—he's managed to track down Mother's dress and Holly is going to wear it when they get married!'

'Er, that's wonderful,' said Amber, since some kind of enthusiastic response was clearly expected.

'And that's not all! She's invited us—that's me *and* you—to her wedding. Isn't that nice? She's getting married to Luke, at Easter.'

Amber blinked. 'But why *me*? She doesn't even know me! I've never even *met* the woman!'

'I know.' Ursula gave a low laugh. 'But she's a real romantic—you'd love her, Amber, I know you would. And she feels that we're all linked through the wedding dress. Which we are, really! And she wants you to be there.'

'Well, it's very sweet of her, but I'll have to write and tell her that I can't go.'

'Can't you?' Ursula's voice was soft. 'Really?'

Amber gave a shaky sigh. 'Of course I can't. Up until a few weeks ago I was planning my own wedding. It would be too much like rubbing salt into the wound. You do understand that, don't you, Ursula?'

'You know I do.'

'Just find out where and when I'm to meet Finn—and tell him that I have only one condition.'

'And that is?'

'That he comes alone.'

'Yes,' said Ursula thoughtfully. 'I'll tell him that.'

Spring had come late to England—it was already April and yet the fields were still a spectrum of different yellows painted by the blaze of daffodils. Every single shade was represented, from the palest clotted cream, through delicate primrose—to the deepest and most vibrant saffron. Amber drove along the country lanes and tried not to be distracted by their sunshine beauty.

The buds on the trees were coyly revealing their shiny green undergarments as the first leaves began to peep through. In a week or two, the lanes would be literally dazzling as the sunlight illuminated the foliage to a lime-coloured brilliance, but for the time being the buds merely hinted at the splendours to come.

Amber changed gear as a hare lolloped like quicksil-

ver across her path. Spring happened in a flash—the
world transformed in a matter of weeks—just as her
whole world had been transformed.

And now she was going to say her goodbyes.

At least, she presumed that was the reason why Finn
wanted to see her. It was in his nature to tidy things up,
to leave no loose ends. He would want to rationalise
their relationship, and the effect it had had on both their
lives. Maybe even to celebrate what they had shared together, while never losing sight of the fact that he, at
least, had decided it was time to move on.

In fact, she could see the logic behind such thinking
herself, if she was forcing herself to *think* logically—not
easy, given her current mental state of trying not to focus
on a whole lifetime without him.

Finn was good at compartmentalising. When she had
first gone to work for him, he had regarded her as strictly
off limits. Indeed, when the attraction between them had
grown so that it could no longer be denied, or hidden,
he had told her that it would probably be better if she
found another job. That business and pleasure rarely
mixed.

She had refused.

Maybe if she had not done so then she would still be
with him today. Maybe she had been wrong to want to
share all his world.

She negotiated a mini-crossroads and slowed down
along the narrow lane until she found the address which
Finn had sent via Ursula. A winding drive eventually led
to a beautiful contemporary building which was only
visible as Amber came round the bend. It was a long,
low construction, composed mainly of glass, from what
Amber could make out—since it blended in so well with
the surrounding countryside.

It had been built amid a natural copse of trees, but

planned so sympathetically that the building seemed almost to *grow* out of the trees, and yet there were wide paths leading to it, lined with curving shrubs of contrasting foliage, and beneath the shrubs poked mauve and white crocuses.

Amber parked and locked her hire car, and made her way towards the front entrance, aware of the sound of tentative birdsong all around her—the surest indication that spring really *was* on its way. Normally, such a sound would have lifted her spirits to the skies. But not today.

Automatic glass doors glided open as she stopped in front of the building, and she stepped into the airy atrium of the interior where a receptionist was seated behind a desk. A cut-glass bowl of hyacinth and freesia stood on the desk in front of her, filling the air with a heady scent.

The receptionist looked up and smiled. 'Hello,' she said.

'Hello.' Amber smiled back. Smiling still did not come naturally, but it was getting easier all the time. 'I'm looking for Finn Fitzgerald.'

The receptionist didn't even need to consult a list, because she smiled even wider and nodded. 'Yes. He's expecting you. He asked me to take you into the Garden Room—he'll be along shortly.'

Same old Finn, thought Amber wryly, as she followed the woman towards the Garden Room. So memorable that just the mention of his name was enough to cause women's eyes to light up. Maybe, she thought, with a welcome trace of dark humour—maybe her life would be simpler without him. She could find a man who would love her and cherish and care for her—and she could do all those things back. But a man whom women wouldn't flutter to be close to. A man who would cause this receptionist to frown, and consult her book and say, 'I *think* he's registered. Let me just check.'

An ordinary man—who wouldn't be dealing with the fantasies of pubescent models and their oversexed mothers on a daily basis!

'Here we are.' The receptionist signalled the room with her hand.

The Garden Room was appropriately named, since it was almost entirely constructed of glass, and the trees and bushes created a living landscape right outside. Violin music was playing softly in the background, while more glass bowls filled with flowers were dotted around the place—some scented, some colourful—and Amber was aware that whoever had designed this room had done so to appeal exclusively to the senses.

She shivered. She would have preferred somewhere Spartan, somewhere with tinny music and bright strip lighting. Why on earth had she let Finn choose the venue?

Because Finn had insisted. The way he always insisted.

'Can I fetch you anything?' the receptionist was saying. 'Some tea or coffee, perhaps? Or wine?'

Amber shook her head. She didn't want him to find her settled down for the day—all cosy and nesting and pouring cups of tea. 'No, thanks,' she said. 'I'm fine.'

After the receptionist had gone, she picked up a magazine, dispassionately noting that her hands were shaking. She read an article on mistresses, surprising herself by becoming completely immersed in the paragraph which was subtitled, 'IS YOUR MAN STRAYING? THE TEN TELL-TALE SIGNS.' If only she had read this before Christmas! Then she would have realised the danger of tell-tale sign number two: 'He *says* he's working!'

How naive she had been! Or how stupid?

All the 'help' he had insisted that Karolina and her mother needed. All the times he had told her he was 'working late'. It was so corny! So predictable! And so unlike the way she'd thought a man like Finn would operate. She had credited him with a little more imagination than that! And a little more honesty, she remembered, with a hurt which still kicked into her aching heart like a mule.

She was so deep in her thoughts that the familiar voice which penetrated them made her briefly close her eyes with despair as she accepted that her heart was thundering like a gun salute.

'Amber?'

She opened her eyes to find that she did not have to look up to stare into that beautiful face of his, because it was almost on a level with hers. But it took a moment or two for it to sink in that Finn was in a wheelchair.

CHAPTER ELEVEN

STUPIDLY, in spite of everything which had happened between them—despite Finn's obvious determination to replace her in his affections with Birgitta—Amber's first instinct was to put her arms around him and hug him. And then to lean across and kiss that delectable mouth of his as she had kissed it so often in the past.

Just seeing him again made her acutely aware of how much she had missed him. His smile. The way he'd made her laugh. Made her mad. Made her *think*. But how long was it since they'd enjoyed all the simple pleasures of a live-in relationship? Not since Allure had shot into the public consciousness and the money mar-kets had started buzzing with talk about when it might go public... Come to think of it—Allure's rapid rise in popularity was probably the reason why she had been asked to do the *Wow!* piece in the first place.

She wondered if her gaze was hungry as it raked over him, and it took her only seconds to realise that he did not look very different at all. Sometimes a wheelchair seemed to diminish a person—the disability crushing and shrinking the personality. But Finn looked just as glowing and as vibrant as he had ever done. Though perhaps a little paler than was usual, she conceded—and the pallor made his eyes emerald-bright and intense.

She struggled to find the words which would neither pity nor condemn him. 'You might have warned me,' she told him wryly.

His laughter had not changed, either. That was as deep and as velvety-irresistible as it had ever been. 'Why?'

he mocked. 'Would you have brought a bib for me to dribble down?'

She heard the unaccustomed bitterness in his voice and wondered what prejudice he had had to suffer since the wheelchair had held him its prisoner.

'You don't look like you're dribbling to me,' she observed candidly.

'No? Maybe I just lick it all away?' he queried huskily, his eyes flashing dark with pure sexual challenge, and Amber was horrified to find her breasts prickling with an urgent desire to have him lick *them*, until she remembered Birgitta.

'Do you?' she questioned, forcing her smile to remain noncommittal as she tore her eyes away from him and looked around the room, and at the way she had come in.

Now she noticed the discreet ramps placed here and there—and it dawned on her that she had seen no stairs anywhere.

'What is this place?' she asked him suddenly.

'It's a retreat,' he answered slowly. 'Started up about ten years ago by a man with vision—an ex-racing driver whose legs were smashed to pieces. A luxurious retreat, where people can take pleasure in their surroundings and do most of the things which able-bodied people take for granted—only without the damning "Disabled" signs to highlight their differences.'

'Oh,' said Amber faintly. 'And what if I'd rung up? And found out first?'

'I asked them not to tell you anything,' he answered smoothly.

His calm and confident assurance riled her. 'Still the control freak, huh, Finn? Still running the world to suit yourself—despite the wheelchair?'

He let out a low sigh. 'My God,' he breathed in admiration. 'You certainly don't pull your punches, do you, O'Neil?'

It was like those early days come alive all over again—the uncomplicated office banter which had grown into real compatibility. 'Why? Did you expect me to, Fitzgerald?' she retorted, finding some solace in the comfort of old nicknames. 'Because you can't get out of that thing to fight me back?'

'Want to fight me, do you, baby?' he taunted softly.

She felt sexual excitement pooling and moistening her, its unexpectedness almost as intoxicating as the feeling itself, a feeling she had imagined was lost to her for ever. But she ruthlessly swamped it down. He might be in a wheelchair, but he had still cheated on her and rejected her. Still written that bald little note. 'Not in the way you think,' she answered coolly.

'And what way is that?'

She shook her head. 'Damn you, Finn Fitzgerald!' she bit out. 'I'm not going to grant you any concessions just because you happen to be…to be…'

'Paralysed?' he put in helpfully.

She didn't like the word. She didn't like the hungry kind of way he was looking at her, either… She didn't like the way he was making her feel… 'Where's Birgitta?' she demanded.

There wasn't a flicker of anything resembling regret on his face, merely a bland kind of smile which stayed firmly in place. His eyes looked very green at that moment. 'I haven't seen Birgitta.'

'Oh? Because you're *paralysed*?' She forced herself to say the word, and as soon as she did her dislike and fear of it dissolved. It was just a word, after all… 'Is that it? You're not the man she thought you were—the man she thought she was getting? The big, hunky stud, Finn Fitzgerald? Well, it's a good thing you weren't able to marry her, isn't it? Or that would have quickly made a mockery of the vows ''in sickness and in health''!'

'Have you quite finished?' he asked her calmly.

'Finished?' She looked at him incredulously. She had spent far too long thinking about the way he'd mistreated her to *ever* stop! 'I haven't even crossed the starting line yet, buster! So what did you decide?' She drew in a deep breath of determination. 'Huh? What went through that cheating mind of yours, Finn? Oh, Lord—Birgitta has done a runner, so who can I turn to? Who could I always turn to? Who loved me enough to come running whenever I clicked my fingers? Sweet little Amber, that's who!'

'And do you? Love me enough, sweet little Amber?'

'Oh, you can go to hell, Finn!' she returned hotly. 'And don't try and use any sympathy I might have for your predicament to get you a declaration of my undying love!'

He pursed his lips into a whistle, in the way he'd used to when she was wearing something very tight. Or wearing nothing at all. 'If that's your idea of sympathy, honey,' he told her drily, 'I think I'll pass.'

Amber looked at him, some of her anger spent, thinking that his physical helplessness made little difference to the way she thought about him as a man. A strong, scheming and gorgeous man! 'So where is Birgitta?'

He shrugged with a big, tensing movement of his shoulders. 'Would you believe it if I told you that I don't know?'

'No, I wouldn't! You must have *some* idea?'

His smile was curiously devoid of any apparent guilt, thought Amber crossly. In fact, *now* he was smiling lazily.

'She's probably having breakfast somewhere,' he remarked.

'At two in the afternoon?'

'It isn't two in the afternoon in the States—and that's where she is.'

'What's she doing there?' asked Amber suspiciously.

'Accompanying Karolina on a modelling job, like she usually does.'

Amber pursed her lips together. 'And you would be there with her, I suppose—if she hadn't been put off by your illness?'

For the first time, his face showed something of his own frustration and anger and fear. 'Don't make judgments on how Birgitta would or would not have responded to my illness.' His voice softened. 'Actually, whatever the state of my health, I would not be in the States with Birgitta for the simple reason that her husband would not like it. They're back together, you see.'

'Really?'

Their eyes met.

'Really.' He nodded.

'Then how did he feel about you necking on top of the piano with her?'

Their gazes remained locked, and countless conflicting emotions flowed across the space between them. Amber felt torn between tears and, impossibly, a sudden desire to laugh.

'That wasn't a very smart thing for me to do,' he admitted slowly.

'No?' Amber affected shocked surprise. 'Kissing another woman in full view of the world and your fiancée wasn't *smart*? What an earth has brought you round to that earth-shattering conclusion?'

'I owe you an explanation,' he growled.

'Or six.'

His eyes narrowed as they focussed on her face. 'You look tired.'

'Well, don't sound so astonished!' she snapped. 'It's hardly surprising, is it?' She glanced back at him, deciding there and then that, whatever had happened between them—and no matter what happened tomorrow or the next day—she would never make allowances for him simply because he happened to be in a wheelchair. Never. 'You, on the other hand,' she told him candidly, 'look disgustingly healthy!'

'Why, thank you,' he answered gravely, and then a wide smile broke out.

'Have I said something funny?' she wanted to know.

He shook his head. 'No. But you're the only person who has dared tell me I look healthy! Most people seem unable to use the word in conjunction with someone in a wheelchair.'

He stole another glance at her, and Amber saw him give a fierce frown of concentration, as he had so often done in the past when he was having difficulty keeping his thoughts focussed. Usually when he wanted her...

'Shall we go over by the French windows?' he asked.

Amber opened her mouth to ask him if he wasn't comfortable where he was, then thought better of it. He clearly wanted to move, and it wasn't for her to question his reasons.

It was the first time she had seen him manipulate the chair, and she'd expected to be shocked, or saddened. Or both. And maybe, if she was being completely honest with herself, then perhaps she was—just a little. But her overriding emotion was one of admiration. He operated it as though he'd spent his life doing nothing else, and, being Finn, managed to turn the movement into something approaching sheer grace and symmetry.

She waited until he had positioned himself by the windows, and then walked towards him very slowly and deliberately, searching his face for signs of resentment at the fact that *she* was still able-bodied, but there were none. Just that easy and appreciative sweeping stare, and the only too familiar glint in the depths of his eyes which normally meant that he was thinking very strongly about one thing. And Amber found herself wondering... wondering...

'Why, you're blushing, Amber,' he murmured as she sat down opposite him.

'And I'm waiting.'

'What are you waiting for, honey?'

She ignored the teasing sensuality she saw written on his face, the honeyed pause in his words. 'For that explanation you just promised me, Finn. Don't tell me you've forgotten already. Maybe I should remind you.' She levelled an accusing stare at him. 'Your affair with Birgitta should do for starters—'

'There was never any affair with Birgitta!' he growled immediately.

'No? Just a little heavy petting, perhaps?' She narrowed her eyes with the intention of shocking him. 'A little non-penetrative sex?' she suggested daringly, and saw fury fall on his face like a dark cloud.

'Amber!' he exploded. 'What the hell's got into you?'

All her anger and her bitterness came pouring out of her mouth like bile. 'I wonder you have the nerve to even *ask* me that!' she stormed. 'How do you think it felt to see you sprawled all over the top of the piano?'

'Don't you think I didn't know how it would feel?'

'Then why *do* it? Why hurt me that way—?'

'Because you wouldn't leave me,' he cut across her, his sigh like a heavy burden. 'You just wouldn't go. I had to take desperate measures because it was a desperate situation. I'd been as cool and offhand and abrupt to you as I knew how—yet still you loved me more than I deserved. Still you wouldn't go.'

The starkness of his words was like being sandbagged. Amber sagged as she stared at him, gripping her hands together so tightly that her knuckles whitened. 'What are you talking about?' she demanded, her voice a hoarse whisper. 'I don't understand.'

'We'd been arguing for weeks. Do you remember?'

'How could I ever forget?' she asked bitterly.

'I'd been working so hard I was threadbare. I was tetchy, impatient—'

'I know,' she put in quietly. 'I was there.'

'Yes.' His eyes softened as he looked at her. 'Then I came back from Australia feeling ill.'

'You *were* ill in Australia,' she pointed out.

He nodded. 'With a virus. The doctors think I was susceptible because I was so wiped out. That's what caused—' with outstretched fingers he indicated his motionless legs '—this.' He looked up at her, from beneath eyelashes which had never looked so sinfully long. Or so dark. 'How much do you know about my illness?'

She'd read everything she could lay her hands on, and knew that Finn had been desperately unlucky in his extreme reaction to the virus. 'I know that it's a post-viral syndrome with varying degrees of severity.' She lifted her chin and looked at him steadily. 'But I don't want to talk about your illness.'

'You don't?'

'Oh, I'm not avoiding the subject because it's too uncomfortable to tackle,' she explained. 'I'd just rather talk about why you kissed Birgitta instead.'

Something in her words seemed to amuse him. 'You never cease to amaze me with your unpredictability, Amber.'

'Why the surprise?' she asked.

'Because when you have some kind of disability like this, you *become* that disability—and that's all people *do* want to talk about. As if they can't see you in isolation from your illness. At least—' and he quirked a smile in her direction '—most people. But not you.'

It was the second time that afternoon that he had paid her a fairly hefty compliment, but Amber was determined not to be swayed by his flattery. 'I'm still waiting, Finn.'

It was a moment or two before he began to speak. 'When I got back to England from the Australian trip, I began to experience odd sensations—a numbness in my toes, and my fingers—and just a general weakness. Everything—even the simplest task—seemed to take the most gigantic effort. Some instinct told me that these symptoms were more than simply jet-lag, or fatigue—'

'But you didn't tell me about them?' she interrupted.

He shook his head. 'No.'

'Why not?'

Their eyes met. 'Instinct again. I sensed that something was seriously wrong. I saw three doctors—all of them experts in their field—and the one tentative diagnosis that they were all prepared to make was that I might be in the early stages of Guillain-Barré syndrome.'

'But that still doesn't explain—'

He shook his head impatiently. 'By New Year's Eve, when I took myself off to see Dr Number Three, I was feeling pretty rough. He wanted to admit me to hospital that night, but I wouldn't let him. So he told me to go home and rest. Quietly...'

Amber knew in Finn-speak 'pretty rough' meant unbearably ill. 'That's why you kept me out of the flat that day?' she hazarded. 'Why you got the professionals in to organise the party? Why you encouraged me to stay at Ursula's?'

He nodded, and something written in his eyes made

her realise just what else he had done. He had used the ultimate deterrent...

'So the kiss—' she spoke slowly '—with Birgitta. It wasn't for real, was it? None of it. It was just a set-up?'

He nodded again. 'That's right. I had come so close to telling you the truth about my illness that night. You were being so sweet, so understanding... I knew that my supposed desire for another woman would be the only sure-fire way I could get you to leave me. You'd as good as told me so yourself.'

She looked at him in bewilderment. 'But *why*, Finn? Why should I have ever wanted to leave you when you most needed me?'

'Because my symptoms were escalating with such rapid speed that I knew from what I had been told by the medics that I was one of those most likely to have a poor outcome from the disease.'

'You mean you might have died?'

'I might.'

'And didn't you think I deserved to make that decision for myself? Don't you think I would have stayed with you—no matter what?'

'I didn't want you to stay with me "no matter what"!' he told her quietly, his eyes shining with intensity. 'I didn't want you to have to dress me. Feed me. Clean me,' he added ruthlessly, searching her face for appalled distaste, but there was none. 'I didn't want you to tie yourself to a cripple for the rest of your life!'

'But you're a cripple now,' she told him with a candour which surprised even herself. 'So what happened to change your mind?'

His eyes narrowed in disbelieving respect. 'I don't believe you, Amber O'Neil. I just don't believe you—'

Amber shook her head. 'I don't want your praise at

the moment, thank you, Finn,' she said firmly. 'I want you to tell me about the night of your party.'

'Okay.' He ran his fingers thoughtfully along the arm of the chair. 'I had practised the two piano pieces very little, but somehow I thought I would get through it— God knows how, when I was feeling as weak as cotton wool. I sat down at the piano—'

'I remember,' she said, shivering.

'And all of a sudden I realised that I *couldn't use my fingers properly*! The reality was like being hit very hard with a sledgehammer—and that was when I kissed Birgitta.'

'And she kissed you back,' Amber observed painfully.

'Yes.' He looked at her from between narrowed eyes. 'It didn't turn me on at all, you know. Not in the slightest.'

'And is that supposed to be some kind of consolation?'

He considered this. 'I think that *I* would find it consoling, if the situation were reversed.'

'But you've no idea whether I've kissed anyone since we've been separated.'

'No.' A pause. 'Have you?'

'No—and you can wipe that smug expression off your face, Finn Fitzgerald!'

'Yeah.' His face became serious once more. 'After you'd left, I got Birgitta to call the doctor, and I was admitted to hospital.'

'And the note?' she questioned. 'The note Birgitta gave to me at the hospital?'

He winced. 'Writing it was the hardest thing I've ever had to do—both mentally *and* physically. I made her promise to give it to you. She didn't want to.'

'Why not?'

'Because she thought you loved me enough to be able to bear the truth.'

'But you didn't?' asked Amber slowly.

'Of course I did! I just didn't want to put you in that position.'

'Until now?'

'Until now,' he echoed.

'And what happened to change your mind?'

'I missed you,' he said simply.

Three words; just three words—but they told her everything she needed to know. She rose to her feet, her mouth a curving smile as she moved to stand in front of him. 'Tell me, Finn,' she urged softly. 'Tell me that in your heart you don't really want me, and I'll go away and never come back again. But if you ask me whether I want you—then the answer remains constant. Because I do. Whether you're stuck in that chair, or out of it. It doesn't go away, the wanting. I'm stuck with it, I guess.'

She saw the starry light which gleamed so green in his eyes, and she bent her face to his to whisper, 'And I don't want your gratitude, either, Finn. I just want you. Whatever you've got to give to me—I want it.'

'Maybe I have nothing to give you?' He looked at her deliberately.

'I don't believe you,' she husked. 'There's been desire written in your eyes since you came in here today. And not just in your eyes, either.' She dropped her gaze provocatively, and let her eyes linger on the butting ridge which was easily visible through the cream chinos he wore. She saw his mouth tighten with tension in response. 'I'm going to make the earth move for you, Finn—even if your feet can't.'

He threw back his head and laughed with uninhibited joy. 'Oh, sugar,' he breathed, with a pleasure which sounded newly minted.

'So why don't we go some place quiet and find out just what we *can* do?' she purred.

He smiled. 'I guess this means that you're going to dominate me sexually from now on, does it?'

'Would that be a problem, then?'

'How could a secret fantasy I've nurtured since I first took your innocence ever be a problem, honey?'

'You may have taken my innocence,' she told him softly, 'but you gave me so much in its place. You taught me everything I know, and now I'm going to demonstrate what a wonderful teacher you were. I want to lick every inch of you, until you're begging me to stop,' she whispered.

'Sweet Lord!' he husked. *'Amber!'*

'Take me somewhere,' she told him, suddenly urgent. 'Somewhere private.'

She saw exquisite anticipation harden his features into a rigid mask as he nodded and released the brake on the chair, moving away so quickly that she had to quicken her pace to keep up with him. Even in physical confinement he was formidable! Amber watched the back of his head with pride as she followed him, and right at that moment he stopped, and turned his head to look at her, and the dark, rugged profile was more heart-stoppingly beautiful than she had ever seen it.

'No regrets?' he asked her softly.

She owed him nothing less than the truth. 'Some,' she admitted quietly. 'It wouldn't be natural if I didn't. But they're disappearing even as I look into your eyes.'

He seemed about to say something then, but clearly thought better of it as he pushed open the door he had stopped outside and wheeled himself in, with Amber close behind.

It was a vast, airy room in which stood the biggest bed Amber had ever seen. It was covered in a midnight-blue throw of rich velvet, and the gold squashy cushions scattered over it gave the room a luxurious, sybaritic look.

He moved round to face her and impulsively she crouched down so that their faces were once more on a level, and she kissed him.

Afterwards, Amber thought it was probably the most perfect kiss that they had ever shared—but then they had been through a lot to get where they were right then. The brush of his mouth was tender, the wet flicker of his tongue both erotic and loving. Oh, so loving.

Amber sighed and put her arms on his shoulders and, long minutes later, after the kiss had ended and they finally came up for air, she put her mouth close to his ear and whispered, 'Finn?'

His voice was almost slurred with pleasure. 'Amber?' he murmured throatily.

'Shall we go to bed now? You'll...' she felt oddly shy, but was determined not to shirk the practicalities of their situation '...have to show me what to do,' she finished breathlessly.

There was a strained, but oddly triumphant note in his answering response. 'Go over there and take your jacket off,' he instructed sultrily. 'And I'll show you everything you need to know.'

Something in his eyes silenced the question she had been about to ask, and Amber walked over to the bed. She began to slowly unbutton the navy cashmere jacket of her trouser suit, just as he had asked, watching him all the time as she did so, wondering whether he wanted her to perform an erotic striptease. Wondering whether that would help him... And wondering, with all these high emotions swirling in the air around them, whether she would be able to do it with any degree of skill.

She took the jacket off and folded it carefully with

fingers which were trying not to shake as she put it down neatly on the bed. Underneath she wore a thin silk camisole and she shivered, more from nerves than from cold. But as she watched him for some kind of reaction, she blinked in astonishment. The unbelievable was happening. Finn was...Finn was...was...

Amber shook her head as he rose from the chair, certain that she must be hallucinating. But, no, hallucinations were supposed to give you a distorted feeling of unreality, and this was real enough.

He took a step towards her which didn't even falter, and that told her something else which her shocked brain was too befuddled to interpret.

It wasn't until he was almost by her side that the truth kicked in, and she slid onto the floor into the welcome arms of oblivion.

CHAPTER TWELVE

AMBER opened her eyes to find that she had been lifted onto the bed.

How?

And Finn was bending over her, his face a picture of frowning concern as he smoothed the hair back from her face.

Flapping her hand at him as though it had been burnt, she attempted to sit up at the same time, but he laid a restraining hand on her bare shoulder.

'Don't move, honey,' he instructed huskily, as he stroked at the skin there with the fleshy pad of his thumb. 'You've had a shock.'

It was so long since she had felt him touch her that instinct almost made her do as he asked, to just luxuriate in that first contact, but then she remembered. And how! With an almighty effort, she wriggled her shoulder free of his hand and sat up, scarcely believing what had happened. What he had *done*!

'Too right I've had a shock,' she agreed shakily, as she drew in a struggling breath of control. 'A shock to know that I could still feel *anything* for a lying, cheating bastard like *you*, Finn Fitzgerald!' She looked at the muscular bunching of his thighs and realised that this was not a man who had spent the past weeks in a wheelchair. *He* must have lifted her onto the bed—and she was no featherweight! 'How long is it since you've been able to walk?'

'About a month,' he admitted. 'I've been building my strength back up.'

'How *could* you, Finn?' she demanded, her question wobbling precariously. 'How could you *deceive* me like that?'

'Because I had to know!' he declared in a low undertone which trembled with a raw passion. He pointed at the empty wheelchair. 'That could so easily have been the outcome of my illness.'

'So?'

'So I needed to know whether you would still want me and desire me if I didn't happen to fit your stereotype of the perfect lover.'

She stared at him in disbelief. Then shook her head. 'A test of my love for you?' she queried acidly. 'Is that what this whole *charade* was for?'

'I *was* paralysed,' he gritted out. 'And I *was* confined to that damned wheelchair.'

'Which doesn't explain why you deceived me!' Her mouth began to wobble again. 'In such a cruel way as that!'

'Doesn't it?' he queried. 'Can't you understand, Amber, that this is so nearly how it *might* have been? This might have been our reality. Being physically disabled is no picnic, you know—'

'I didn't say it was,' she said stubbornly. 'But you knew that I loved you.'

'You loved me when I was able-bodied,' he argued. 'That's the man you took on. But things had changed—more dramatically than I would ever have wished for. I didn't want to take advantage of that love by tying you to a man you would have to help feed, wash—a man who might not have been able to give you the babies that I know you've always longed for.'

'But you're none of those things,' she objected. 'So why trick me?'

'It wasn't a question of *tricking* you, sweetheart,' he

said, in the gentlest voice she had ever heard him use. 'But don't you think that it would have always been there, like a great big barrier between us, this huge question?'

'Of whether I loved you enough to stay with you if you *had* ended up in a wheelchair?'

'That's one way of looking at it.' A small frown pleated his forehead. 'But how about if I told you that I *didn't* doubt your loyalty or your love or your steadfastness, not for a moment—though I wasn't sure whether you would still desire me. And that maybe I wanted to have the opportunity to see you demonstrate all those things, and more...and you did...' His eyes softened with green luminosity as they met hers in a long look. 'Oh, and you did, Amber—beyond my wildest imaginings. You made me feel normal again—even though I was in a wheelchair. No one else could do that, honey.'

He moved to brush a lock of golden hair away from her face, and just the touch of him was as potent as it had ever been, but with trembling fingers she pushed him away, shaking the silken fall of hair in denial.

'No! You mustn't touch me.' She nearly said, Not yet, but clamped her lips tightly together before the traitorous words could escape.

He gave a lazy smile. 'Honestly?'

'Honestly,' she told him, but she didn't quite trust herself—not when he was standing so close to her—so she gingerly got up off the bed and walked over to the other side of the room.

'Amber.' He spoke softly.

Amber turned round, wincing slightly at the bizarre circumstances of their situation. How the bed mocked her now. She had been so eager for his touch that she had been planning the best way to remove her clothes. When all the time... She looked into his eyes. 'What?'

'Tell me what you're feeling.'

She realised how they had lost some of their ability to communicate in the past months. How work and living had swallowed up everything so that there never seemed any time left. It was as though, once they had declared their love for each other, they had decided that no more work needed to be done on the relationship. And maybe now it was too late...

'I'm feeling betrayed, if you must know. And disturbed by your obvious need to control me...*yes*!' She saw the denial in his eyes and spoke before he could interrupt her. '*Control* me, Finn! And please don't look so shocked. You wouldn't tell me the truth about your illness, and you wouldn't tell me the truth about your recovery! You've manipulated and played with my feelings—'

'And I've explained why! I did it mainly to *protect* you!'

'That doesn't make it any better, Finn! I'm supposed to be your partner and your equal—not some child to be protected!' she retorted. 'But even if your behaviour concerning your illness was understandable—chivalrous, even—your need to control me has been going on for as long as you've known me.'

'Oh, has it?' He leaned back against the wall at that, with a gesture which managed to be provocative and casual at the same time, and her first thought was that he might be using his considerable sexual power to entice her into letting her anger just slide. It wasn't until afterwards that Amber wondered whether or not he might have been feeling weary—because the fact remained that he *had* been a very sick man... 'I'm sure you've got a whole list of examples,' he drawled.

'Too right I have!' She regarded him steadily. 'There was the way you tried to get me to resign from Allure, when you realised that your feelings for me were growing—'

'Because I didn't believe that we could have a successful partnership professionally *and* personally—I explained that! I thought that one or the other would suffer.'

'And you didn't want to risk your beloved business, I suppose?' she challenged.

He shook his dark head. 'I didn't want to risk my relationship with you,' he refuted. 'But it was all academic anyway, because you wouldn't resign, would you, Amber?'

'No,' she agreed, and saw him smile. It was a ruthlessly melting smile, but Amber steeled herself against its power. 'And anyway—' she looked up at him from beneath the shadow cast by her lashes '—I proved you wrong, didn't I?'

'Yeah, you proved me wrong,' he echoed softly. 'You keep proving me wrong every step of the way, Amber O'Neil. Every barrier I've ever erected, you just swipe it right down.'

Amber locked her lips together. 'I'm not through yet!' she told him fiercely. 'You wouldn't let me take the Cassini contract, either—would you?' she reminded him, but he shook his head.

'Oh, no, honey—you're not laying *that* at my feet. *You* were the one who decided not to accept the contract—'

'Because you told me that our relationship was likely to suffer—'

'And that much was true.'

'Well, why didn't you give me the opportunity to find out for myself?' she demanded.

'The opportunity was there for the taking—you could have gone right ahead and accepted the job,' he pointed out. 'But what if I'd pretended that we *could* just carry on as normal—knowing how difficult it would be to sustain a relationship with you jetting all over the world? What then?' His eyes blazed out their question as he stared hard at her.

'You're a grown woman, Amber!' he continued. 'And a responsible woman. You couldn't just have opted out of a binding contract because it kept you away from your boyfriend! Think what that would have done for your reputation! Your pride. Everything we'd worked for.' He gave a heavy sigh. 'God, I'm damned if I tell you the truth and damned if I don't, aren't I? Just what do you want from me, Amber O'Neil?'

She felt tears begin to slide down her cheeks. 'I don't know any more,' she whispered brokenly, but it wasn't quite the truth, and Finn was far too astute not to pick up on that.

'So if I came over there to comfort you, would you accuse me of taking advantage?' he mused.

'No.'

'Or trying to control you?'

She shook her head. 'No.'

'What if I tried to kiss you?'

She stared at him from between wet lashes. 'I think I'd kiss you back.'

'And do you think you'd enjoy it?'

'I think so.'

'In spite of everything that's happened?'

'Maybe because of everything that's happened,' she said, in a snuffly kind of voice. 'Because I never felt this nervous the first time you kissed me.'

'Nor me,' he admitted.

They stared at one another, and then he crossed the room and opened his arms to her, and she went straight into them without hesitation, like a bird flying in from the ravages of the storm.

'Oh, Finn!' she sobbed, and felt the wetness of his own tears against her cheek. *'Finn!'*

'I know,' he soothed shakily. 'Believe me, I know.'

It was several minutes—maybe longer—before he led her over to the bed and drew her down beside him, and as he began to reacquaint himself with her body she thought that he had never been this reverential, or this tender, before. His fingertips travelled over her face with wonder, seeking out each pore of her skin with the feather-light sensitivity of a blind man exploring new and wonderful territory.

And for Amber it felt like the first time all over again—only better. Deeper, and somehow more sacred. But then they had come a long way to get where they were at that precise moment. She had been many things to Finn—his virgin lover, his assistant, his fiancée—but she couldn't ever remember feeling quite this much his *equal* before.

Never had his body felt so delicious next to hers as they laid each other bare. Just the sensation of his skin brushing warmly against hers felt so heart-stoppingly intimate that she felt she might die with the pleasure. And that was before he had touched her in any way which was at all sexual. Though, quite honestly, just the warmth of his breath against her neck felt like the most loving and erotic feeling she had ever experienced.

She bit down hard on her bottom lip to stop it from trembling, and he must have felt the sudden tension in her, for he turned her face to his and there was a tender question in his eyes.

'What is it?' he whispered.

'This just feels so *amazing*,' she told him softly.

'What does?'

'Holding you.' She tightened her arms around him to demonstrate. 'Being here with you.'

'You're preaching to the converted,' he told her unsteadily as he pushed her hair right back off her face. 'So why the sad face?'

'I just feel I'm poised on the brink of something,' she admitted. 'And I don't know what it is.'

'But you're scared?' he guessed.

'Terrified!'

'Me, too,' he confided softly, and drew her hand across his chest to lay it on the warm skin over his heart. 'Feel.'

She felt the strong but rapid thundering of his heart against her palm and knew that, for all their previous physical compatibility, he felt this sensation of wonder as well. As if they were about to move into a different dimension of love altogether.

He smiled as he lifted her hand away, turned it over and studied it, tracing one of the lines with a long finger.

'And is it a long life?' asked Amber shakily.

'I was reading your heart-line,' he amended, as he bent his dark head with gracious inclination to softly kiss a fingertip.

'And?'

'And it's a very happy line.' His face was serious. 'I'm going to make damned sure of that.'

But she gripped his naked shoulders and shook her head firmly. '*We're* going to make sure of that,' she corrected. 'Our future is a joint responsibility.'

'You make it sound so serious,' he teased.

'Well, it *is* serious,' she agreed. 'And so is *this*.' She smiled with satisfaction as she slithered her hand down his spine to rest possessively on the swell of one hard buttock, and felt him squirm with pleasure.

'That's nice,' he murmured.

She moved her hand round and began to stroke him. 'And this?'

'That's even better,' he told her thickly, and blotted out all the pain with his lips.

CHAPTER THIRTEEN

'OH, AMBER—you look just beautiful,' sighed Ursula.

Amber looked at her wedding-day reflection in the rather spotted mirror provided by the small Irish hotel they were staying in. She and Ursula had been having a whale of a time since they had checked into the Black Bollier three days ago. They had been given the biggest bedroom, breakfast brought to them in bed every morning by the eccentric owner, Alan Bollier, and had been treated to some good, old-fashioned Irish hospitality!

'I *feel* beautiful,' Amber said softly. 'More beautiful than I ever felt in those few modelling jobs I did, where the photographer could always fiddle around with the pictures until you came out looking perfect.'

'You feel beautiful because you're loved so much by Finn?' guessed Ursula, unable to keep the slight trace of envy from her voice.

Amber looked up quickly. 'I didn't mean to crow—'

But Ursula shook her head. 'I know you didn't—and I mean it from the bottom of my heart when I say that I couldn't be happier for you. Both of you.'

'I know that.' Amber looked at the woman who stared back at her. The ivory silk-satin and organza wedding dress flattered her slender frame perfectly. She had let her hair grow, and today it was piled up on top of her head, with the silk-tulle of the veil flowing down around her shoulders like a creamy waterfall.

'And Mother would be so proud to have you wear the dress she bought.' Ursula smiled, but she was blinking rapidly as she said it.

Amber fiddled unnecessarily with the veil. Holly Lovelace had had the dress sent to her just as soon as she and Finn had announced the date of their wedding. 'Did it look different when Holly wore it?' she questioned.

Ursula smiled again. 'Totally. Although you're both red-heads—she has much darker colouring than you. And you're wearing your hair up, and the flowers are different. Holly's in the church with Luke—looking disgustingly glowing and pregnant. She says the dress wouldn't go past her thighs at the moment!'

Amber hesitated. 'And did you...did you invite Ross?'

Ursula seemed to have some kind of lump in her throat, for she took a moment or two to clear it before she spoke. 'Yes, I did, and he said thank you very much, and gave me the most gorgeous present to give you both, but he's not coming.'

'Not even at the last moment?'

Ursula shook her head. 'Not even at the last moment,' she echoed quietly. 'He doesn't really like weddings.'

Amber nodded, and picked her bouquet up, taking a brief moment to close her eyes with enjoyment as she breathed in the heady scent of the flowers. These days, she appreciated each one of her senses, as Finn had always taught her to do, but especially since his illness. She reached out to touch a petal, feeling its velvet softness against her fingertip as she looked at the posy. It was an old-fashioned bouquet—she had copied the one her mother had carried at *her* wedding.

But then Amber and Finn's wedding itself was an old-fashioned affair. Finn's mother was too frail to travel far, and they had chosen to get married in Ireland, in the tiny village church which had married generations of Fitzgeralds.

The church was jam-packed with Fitzgeralds now, and Finn and Ursula had managed to track down various members of the O'Neil family living in Ireland, and had invited them to the wedding. There had been a fine old party at the Black Bollier the previous evening, when Amber and Ursula had discovered cousins they had thought long lost. And meeting some of their father's kin had given both sisters a new feeling of security, and of belonging.

'We'd better go,' said Ursula, with a swift glance at her watch. 'Don't want to keep them waiting too long—the priest won't like it!'

Amber laughed, her heart pattering with nerves and excitement as she looked at her sister, who was wearing a dress and jacket in palest blue silk, with a wide-brimmed hat to match. 'You look beautiful too,' she told Ursula softly. 'No, you *do*,' she added, before Ursula could contradict her. '*Stunning!*'

Ursula smiled. 'Thank you.'

'But I wish you'd agreed to be my bridesmaid,' said Amber wistfully.

'I know you do. And I'm too old and too fat and too much of a realist to want to stand behind my model sister!' came Ursula's truthful reply. 'Besides, it's a far greater honour to give you away—especially as it's usually a man who performs that role.'

And Amber uttered a silent prayer that Ursula would one day find a man of her own—a man she could grow to like and respect and love as much as Ross Sheridan. 'Let's go,' she said.

It was only a short walk to the church from the hotel, on a summer's day that was more blustery than golden, but Amber didn't need sunshine to make her day complete. The sunshine was all in her heart, radiating out of her, she felt as though it were coursing round her veins and spilling onto the ground where she walked.

She had never seen a church so full, and yet the only person she really saw was Finn, standing tall and proud as he waited for her at the altar. Amber paused just for a second to stare at him.

He had sold out his share of Allure to Jackson—and Amber had been neither surprised nor perturbed at his decision. A career he had once seen as exciting now seemed superficial. His illness had changed Finn forever, and he no longer viewed the world in the same way.

He had turned to her one day and declared passionately that, 'I want to do something that *counts*, Amber!'

She had needed no explanation, no justification. 'Then *do* it!' she had urged.

Recognising a man with natural dynamism, the hospital where he'd lain so sick had invited him to sit on the board, and Finn had accepted the honour with pleasure. He also had complicated plans for some of his investment income to benefit charities with which he could identify strongly—and this was also as a direct response to his illness. But, in the wider picture, Amber suspected that the only way Finn could *really* do something which counted would be to enter the political arena... She just didn't want him to ever work himself into the ground again.

Did he sense that she was in the church? Or was he merely impatient to begin? Whatever the reason, he turned round and looked at her, and the emerald light from his eyes dazzled brighter even than the sudden ray of sunlight which shafted in through one of the high windows.

The organist struck up the march and Amber and Ursula exchanged one final glance as they began to walk slowly towards Finn.

Near the back of the church sat Holly and Luke—Holly with her hands folded serenely over her swollen belly.

'Ouch!' she said.

Luke's blue eyes crinkled. 'Baby kicking again?'

'There must be a stronger word than *kicking*,' Holly moaned. 'Pulverising, perhaps. I'm going to end this pregnancy black and blue—I just know I am!'

'Must be a boy,' he observed, with a grin.

'Don't be so sexist!' she reprimanded. 'It could just be an exceptionally strong girl!'

Luke laid his hand over hers and waited until he felt the heel of his unborn child thrusting against the green voile of his wife's dress. 'Have I told you lately how much I love you?' he murmured.

'Well, you have,' Holly whispered. 'But you can keep telling me. Only maybe not right now—because here comes the bride!'

It was a tiny church, and yet the path to Finn seemed to last forever. Afterwards, Amber could scarcely remember saying her vows, remembering only that some of the words had seemed unbearably poignant, especially when they got to the bit about 'in sickness and in health'. Even when he'd slid the simple gold band on her finger it had all seemed a bit of a blur through her tears.

In fact the bit she remembered best was when the priest had cleared his throat and announced, somewhat reluctantly, that, 'You may now kiss the bride.'

Finn had lifted the veil from her face and stared at her for a long moment, and Amber had seen the love shining from his eyes and had known then that, whatever else life threw at them, they would come through it. A lifetime of living and loving with this man.

Now *that* was the best bit!

HARLEQUIN ◆ PRESENTS®

WANTED: ONE WEDDING DRESS

A trilogy by
Sharon Kendrick

Three brides in search of the perfect dress—and the perfect husband!

In February 1999 wedding-dress designer
Holly Lovelace marries the man of her dreams in
One Bridegroom Required!
Harlequin Presents® #2011

In March 1999 Amber has her big day in
One Wedding Required!
Harlequin Presents® #2017

In April 1999 Ursula, Amber's sister,
walks up the aisle, too!
One Husband Required!
Harlequin Presents® #2023

Available wherever Harlequin books are sold.

HARLEQUIN®
Makes any time special ™

HPWOWD

Look for a new and exciting series from Harlequin!

HARLEQUIN *Duets*™

Two <u>new</u> full-length novels in one book, from some of your favorite authors!

Starting in May, each month we'll be bringing you two new books, each book containing two brand-new stories about the lighter side of love! Double the pleasure, double the romance, for less than the cost of two regular romance titles!

Look for these two new Harlequin Duets™ titles in May 1999:

Book 1:
WITH A STETSON AND A SMILE
by Vicki Lewis Thompson
THE BRIDESMAID'S BET
by Christie Ridgway

Book 2:
KIDNAPPED? by Jacqueline Diamond
I GOT YOU, BABE by Bonnie Tucker

2 GREAT STORIES BY 2 GREAT AUTHORS FOR 1 LOW PRICE!

Don't miss it! Available May 1999 at your favorite retail outlet.

HARLEQUIN®
Makes any time special.™

Look us up on-line at: http://www.romance.net

HDGENR

**Race to the altar—
Maxie, Darcy and Polly are**

The HUSBAND *Hunters*

in a fabulous new
Harlequin Presents® miniseries by

LYNNE GRAHAM

These three women have each been left a share of
their late godmother's estate—but only if they marry
withing a year and remain married for six months....

Maxie's story: **Married to a Mistress**
Harlequin Presents #2001, January 1999

Darcy's story: **The Vengeful Husband**
Harlequin Presents #2007, February 1999

Polly's story: **Contract Baby**
Harlequin Presents #2013, March 1999

Will they get to the altar in time?

Available in January, February and March 1999
wherever Harlequin books are sold.

HARLEQUIN®
Makes any time special ™

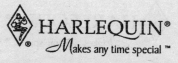

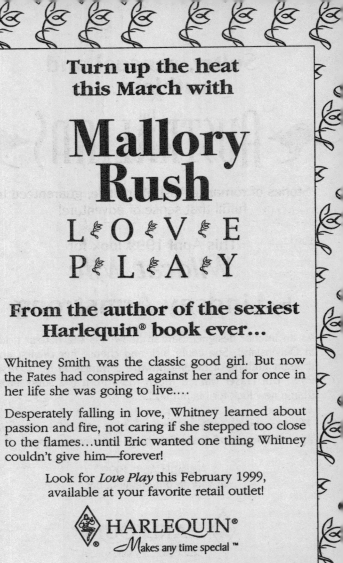

Coming Next Month

HARLEQUIN PRESENTS®

THE BEST HAS JUST GOTTEN BETTER!

#2019 PACIFIC HEAT Anne Mather
Olivia was staying with famous film star Diane Haran to write her biography, despite the fact that Diane had stolen Olivia's husband. Now Olivia planned to steal Diane's lover, Joe Castellano, by seduction...for revenge!

#2020 THE MARRIAGE DECIDER Emma Darcy
Amy had finally succumbed to a night of combustible passion with her impossibly handsome boss, Jake Carter. Now things were back to business as usual; he was still a determined bachelor...and she was pregnant....

#2021 A VERY PRIVATE REVENGE Helen Brooks
Tamar wanted her revenge on Jed Cannon, the notorious playboy who'd hurt her cousin. She'd planned to seduce him, then callously jilt him—but her plan went terribly wrong: soon it was marriage she wanted, not vengeance!

**#2022 THE UNEXPECTED FATHER Kathryn Ross
(Expecting!)**
Mom-to-be Samantha Walker was looking forward to facing her new life alone—but then she met the ruggedly handsome Josh Hamilton. But would they ever be able to overcome their difficult pasts and become a real family?

**#2023 ONE HUSBAND REQUIRED! Sharon Kendrick
(Wanted: One Wedding Dress)**
Ross Sheridan didn't know that his secretary, Ursula O'Neill, was in love with him until his nine-year-old daughter, Katie, played matchmaker.... Then it was only a matter of time before Katie was Ross and Ursula's bridesmaid!

#2024 WEDDING FEVER Lee Wilkinson
Raine had fallen in love with Nick Marlowe, not knowing the brooding American was anything but available. Years later, she was just about to marry another man when Nick walked back into Raine's life. And this time, he *was* single!